WITCH
WATER

WITCH WATER

Phyllis Reynolds Naylor

ILLUSTRATED BY
Gail Owens

A YEARLING BOOK

Published by
Dell Publishing Co.
a division of
The Bantam Doubleday Dell Publishing Group, Inc.
1 Dag Hammarskjold Plaza
New York, New York 10017

Yearling ® TM 913705, Dell Publishing Co., Inc.

ISBN: 0-440-40038-4

Reprinted by arrangement with Macmillan Publishing Company on behalf of Atheneum

Printed in the United States of America

March 1988

10 9 8 7 6 5 4 3 2 1

CW

for Sharon and Bobbi

WITCH
WATER

chapter one

At first Lynn was sure that the old woman waited for her—old Mrs. Tuggle, who kept to herself in the house on the hill. Lynn need only pause for a moment, remembering, and the thin, bony face appeared before her—one eye green, one eye gray, with a mouth that opened a crack when she smiled, displaying a gold tooth. It was the way she looked at Lynn—a sly, calculating kind of squint—as though watching for the proper time to make a move, the right time to draw Lynn under her spell.

There were ties that drew Lynn to Mrs. Tuggle whether she trusted her or not. Mother, for instance, was a writer who rented a remodeled hen house from the old woman to use as a studio. Judith, Lynn's sister, had spent most of her evenings last summer sewing with Mrs. Tuggle in an upstairs room of the ancient house. Stevie, Lynn's small brother, liked the stories Mrs. Tuggle told of bogles and hobyahs, and often wandered up to visit without telling anyone where he was going. And there was a pull deep inside Lynn herself that she couldn't explain. Perhaps it was this that frightened her most.

Autumn was creeping slowly in, bringing a chill in the mornings. Stevie was off to kindergarten, Judith was interested in other things. And now Mrs. Tuggle's small sharp eyes seemed focused not only on Lynn but on her friend Marjorie Beasley, better known as Mouse, as well. No one, however, took Lynn's fears seriously. No one but Marjorie. Lynn's father grew impatient with talk of witchcraft, which he labeled "imaginative nonsense."

Lynn sat at the table, idly balancing her knife on the edge of her plate, wondering if she dared bring up the subject again. Proof. If she only had evidence that the old woman was trying to lure them into her coven—a buried rock, maybe, with the words, "Elnora Tuggle was admitted this day to the circle of sorcery," engraved in Greek letters, and signed below with a big splotch of raven's blood. Something like that. Instead of proof, there was just this awful feeling, this sense of evil, an awesome awareness of being near the un-known. . . .

Surprisingly, however, it was Father who brought the subject up.

"Amazing what ideas people get when they don't have enough to keep them busy," he said, spreading a blob of butter over his mashed potato. "A clerk at the courthouse was checking the graves in the old cemetery with county death certificates, and it seems he can't find a certificate for somebody named C. L. Pritchard. One of the secretaries says it's the grave of Mrs. Tuggle's young brother, drowned over forty years ago when he was sixteen. Now there's gossip going around about how the boy really died. Anything to start a little ex-citement."

The knife on Lynn's plate clunked off the edge and onto the table. She didn't move, her eyes fixed on her father.

Mrs. Morley looked at Lynn and then at her husband. "Now, Dick you're going to get Lynn started again. The last thing we need around here is more gossip about Mrs. Tuggle."

Lynn pressed her lips together firmly, her jaw clenched. Maybe she had good reason to be worried.

"That's exactly why I brought it up," Mr. Morley said. "I want the girls to see how easily gossip can get started and how quickly it gets out of hand. Some-

5

body misfiled the death certificate, obviously, but now there's talk that perhaps this death wasn't accidental, perhaps it was murder, and the missing death certificate would prove it. A lot of nonsense, that's what it is."

"Don't look at me," Judith said from her side of the table. "I'm not the least bit concerned about Mrs. Tuggle. Wait till Lynn starts junior high—she'll have so much to think about, she'll forget all about her witch hobby."

"It's not a hobby!" Lynn snapped angrily. She hadn't said a word, and suddenly they were all jumping on her. "I'll keep my thoughts to myself, thank you, and you can just stop trying to pry inside my mind."

"Hey!" Dad said playfully, "don't get mad. I'm sorry I brought the subject up. It's just that I knew you'd hear the gossip sooner or later, and I wanted you to know how it started."

Stevie sat eating his peas one at a time with his fingers. His eyes, wide-spaced, resembled Mother's. So did Judith's. It was Lynn who looked like her father—pale, gray-speckled eyes in a pale freckled face—a long sort of face that looked as though it had been stretched a little. There were times when she resented looking like her father, and this was one of them.

"I didn't know Lynn's hobby was witches," Stevie said.

"Sure, I collect them and keep them in a bottle."

6

Lynn pushed her plate away and got up.

Father reached over and grabbed her arm, pulling her to him. "C'mon, girl. I didn't mean to ruin dinner," he said fondly. "If I mention Mrs. Tuggle again, may my mouth turn to mush. Buddies?"

"Buddies," Lynn said, not quite convincingly. She went to the small room off the hallway—the music room, they called it, because it held the piano. There was also a bay window on one side, and here Lynn curled up on the cushioned seat—her favorite thinking place. Her thoughts spun wildly.

She shook her head to clear it of "imaginative nonsense." She would go about this scientifically, methodically. She would take each piece of information she had about Mrs. Tuggle and fit it carefully into the puzzle, and she would not make any accusations till the puzzle was complete.

It did not help, of course, that Mother herself was working on a novel about witches. Why had she turned from adventure stories of horses and the high seas to writing about bodily possession, spooking the atmosphere even more? There were times Lynn felt that her mother believed in the strangeness of Mrs. Tuggle also—times when a flicker of fear reflected in Mrs. Morley's eyes as Lynn told her something about the old woman that she hadn't noticed herself.

But the conversation would always end with the

warning that it was easy to accuse someone falsely—
that just because Mrs. Tuggle was a little eccentric
did not mean she was a witch, and that Lynn need
only remember the Salem witch trials to see what care-
less accusations had done to many innocent women.

"Lynn."

Mother was standing in the doorway, her light brown
hair drawn back with a blue scarf. She was holding a
cellophane-wrapped platter of blueberry muffins.

"The best way to deal with suspicions about somebody is to get to know them better," she said. "Just
for me, won't you try to be more friendly with Mrs.
Tuggle? Sometimes, you know, people sense when
others distrust them, and it just builds the wall between them even higher. How about taking her this
platter of fresh muffins?"

It was exactly what Lynn wanted—the opportunity
to observe Mrs. Tuggle up close—to learn everything
she could.

"All right," she said, getting up. "But I'm going to
call Mouse to go with me."

"Fine. Mrs. Tuggle will appreciate it. She gets so
lonely." Mother started back to the kitchen, then
stopped, and her eyes were laughing. "If you're not
back by ten, I'll call the sheriff."

Marjorie Beasley lived two blocks away. Every home

in this section of town was Victorian, with high ceilings and gingerbread ornamentation all around. But the Beasley house was "rather coming apart," as Mother put it, for the paint was peeling, the roof needed shingles, and the porch swing had come down months ago and had not been put back up again.

Mouse, in fact, always looked as though *she* were coming apart—or perhaps that she *had* come apart and someone had thrown her back together again. Her socks often did not match or her shoelaces were too short or her wrinkled tee-shirt had obviously been selected at random and pulled down over any pair of jeans that was handy. More often than not, she simply pulled on a big poncho that came down below her bony knees, and Lynn suspected that she wore nothing underneath but pants. It certainly made dressing easier. To complete her costume, Marjorie wore a huge owllike pair of glasses, and Judith had once remarked that if Mouse ever flapped her arms, she'd fly.

Perhaps Mouse and the Beasley home looked as they did because the family itself was coming apart. Marjorie's two older brothers had married and moved away, and only a few weeks ago her parents had decided to separate. Marjorie's mother had gone to Ohio to live with relatives, and Mouse had stayed behind with her father in the big house on the hill.

Mr. Beasley owned a store that specialized in rare

books. When he came home in the evenings, he helped cook dinner, but the housekeeping was Marjorie's responsibility. If she should be taking blueberry muffins to anyone, Lynn decided, it was the Beasleys. So when Mouse answered the door in a huge orange tee-shirt that came almost to her knees, Lynn said, "Mom sent half these muffins for you, and I'm supposed to take the rest to Mrs. Tuggle. Want to come with me?"

Mouse opened the screen door wide and followed Lynn back to the kitchen. "I don't understand your mother," she said simply. "I really don't. Why is she always trying to get you to go see Mrs. Tuggle? Doesn't she even care what happens?"

Lynn put half the muffins on a plate, then added one extra and wrapped the others up again. "She says that the best way to overcome my suspicions is to get to know her better."

"I'd rather go on being suspicious," Mouse said. "When I'm near her, Lynn, I just feel . . . well, *weak*. Like I'm turning into butter. It's as if something's in the air that I can't see."

"Then *you* feel it too." Lynn perched on a kitchen stool, her tan ponytail hanging down her back, and looked intently at her friend. "I wish it was something we could touch—something we could show to somebody. Dad says it's all imaginative nonsense."

"He wouldn't say that if you went up to Mrs. Tuggle's

some night and never came back." Marjorie picked up a muffin and stuffed part of it in her mouth, catching the crumbs with her other hand.

Lynn smiled faintly. "Mother says if we're not back by ten, she'll call the sheriff. Come on, Mouse. I'll feel better if you're along. Besides, I've got new information. I'll tell you on the way up."

It was unfair, Lynn knew, because there were only two things that could lure Mouse into doing what she didn't want to do—food and secrets, and Lynn had used both for bait. They walked back through the hall, past the book-lined study where Marjorie's father was sorting a box of old magazines.

"Going out for a walk with Lynn," Mouse called, pausing a moment in the doorway.

Mr. Beasley turned and looked at them over glasses that were only half as big as Marjorie's—little half-circles that rested just below his eyes.

"Hi, Lynn," he said. A big mustache seemed to cover his entire mouth and made Lynn wonder idly whether that was what made Mrs. Beasley leave him. It matched the shaggy sideburns on either side of his face as well as his heavy brows. "Been reading about your father in the paper—about that zoning commission that's studying the old cemetery. It said that some folks want to dig it up and build a high rise apartment."

Lynn nodded. Father was a lawyer for the county,

and she didn't pay much attention to what he did. Much of what he talked about at the dinner table didn't particularly interest her. But she knew about the cemetery, and of course there was that bit about the death certificate. . . .

"He was saying something about the cemetery just today," Lynn answered.

Mr. Beasley carefully studied the date on one of the magazines and then laid it in a pile with the others. "Well, I, for one, hope they give up the idea. Every time anything gets to be a hundred years old, seems there's always somebody who wants to tear it down or dig it up or cover it over with cement. This is a fine old Indiana town, and I don't see why we have to look like a spring chicken when we're not. Next you know it'll be all the old houses." He grunted disgustedly. "And then I suppose we'll do away with *people* who reach a hundred."

Lynn didn't quite know how to answer. "Mother sent over some blueberry muffins," she said hesitantly.

Mr. Beasley smiled without looking up. "I'll have one later. Tell her we appreciate it, Lynn. And if you want to tell your Dad how I feel about digging up old cemeteries, I won't mind a bit."

Lynn and Marjorie went out on the porch and started up the brick sidewalk to the house at the top of the hill. Lynn tried to imagine all the homes on the street being replaced by split levels, and a high rise apartment building where the old cemetery was now. That would be absolutely awful, she agreed.

The sky had turned a dusky gray, like smoke settling lower and lower over the treetops. The street lights came on, and lamps burned in windows along the way. The air had a crispness about it that reminded Lynn of apples and dry leaves. For three weeks she and Mouse had been walking up this same hill with books under their arms, but they always made a left turn before they got to the top and walked four blocks to Dover School. Sixth grade at last. It used to be all they ever thought about. Now they thought about Mrs. Tuggle and just what it was she wanted of them.

"Okay," Mouse said finally. "What's the information?"

Lynn remembered. "Tonight . . . at the dinner table," she began slowly, wanting to make it last, "Dad said that a clerk at the courthouse was checking all the graves in the cemetery with county death certificates and there was only one missing . . . C. L. Pritchard."

Mouse wasn't particularly impressed. "What's so interesting about that? I mean, if they had the certificate but the *grave* was missing, now that would be something. Anyway, what's a death certificate, and who's C. L. Pritchard?"

"Well, when somebody dies, a doctor has to sign a paper saying that he examined the body and that it

13

was really dead and he has to write down why the person died, just to make it official. But they can't find one for C. L. Pritchard who just happens to be Mrs. Tuggle's brother."

Mouse stopped and looked at Lynn. "She told us he drowned when he was sixteen."

"That's what she *said*, and that's what everybody believes. But what if a doctor never saw the body? What if he died of something else? What if he was murdered instead?"

Mouse sat down on a low wall along the sidewalk. "That does it," she declared flatly. "I'm not going up there. Look, Lynn, I've got all sorts of things to do tonight. I promised Dad I'd wash my hair, and I've got to write Mother, and the dishes aren't done. . . ."

Lynn sat down beside her. "I'm sorry I said that. Dad says it's all stupid gossip."

"You mean other people are thinking the same thing?"

"Just some of the secretaries at the courthouse. Dad says that's the way stories get started and reputations get ruined."

Mouse shook her head. "No deal. No way. Look, Lynn, I'll go as far as her porch, but then I'm going to wait on the steps till you come out. Okay?"

"Sure," Lynn said, knowing that curiosity would get the better of Mouse and drive her inside. It always did. Marjorie was absolutely terrified and enthralled by suspense. She reached for it and backed away at the same time. She panicked whenever they met Mrs. Tuggle, but would have been furious if Lynn ever went to visit without her. Maybe she just liked to be scared. And maybe that's all there was to it for her, and possibly for Lynn as well. Imaginative nonsense. She frowned. No, there was more involved than that. There was real fear, and she couldn't seem to make Father believe that.

They passed a clump of spruce trees on a corner lot, and instantly Mrs. Tuggle's house came into view, dark against the night sky. A trace of purple remained in the gathering clouds overhead, and the chimney of the old house seemed to reach out from the roof and touch it, like the spire on a church. Tall trees stood like spies in the front yard, their leafy ears turned in all directions, and a thorn apple blocked the front door completely from view. In the vast yard behind, which sloped directly down to the creek, were an old barn, a tractor shed, and the remodeled hen house where Mrs. Morley wrote.

An upper porch extended around three sides of the house like a balcony, with a staircase leading down. The windows were completely dark. There was no light on at all.

"She's not home," Mouse said, relieved. "Let's go back."

Lynn paused. There was no sound but the wind in

the trees. Perhaps the old woman had gone shopping. Perhaps she had gone to bed early and would not want to be disturbed. But suddenly, the door opened slowly and they could see the figure of a small woman beckoning to them.

A light came on behind Mrs. Tuggle, and she opened the screen. She stood there, peering out into the darkness.

"Come on in, girls—the air's nippy, it is. I was about to have my evening tea, and there's water enough for all of us."

"How did she know we were out here?" Mouse whispered.

"I don't know. Maybe she was watching from the window." Lynn started up the steps and, as she knew would happen, Mouse followed obediently.

"We didn't think you were home," Lynn said to Mrs. Tuggle. "The house was dark."

"Eh, I'm not much for lights—till it's really black, you know." Mrs. Tuggle led the way inside. "When you've lived in a house as long as I have, you know where everything is. Don't need a light to tell me where the teapot is, or the cups either. What's this, Lynn girl, muffins?"

"Mother sent them. She baked this afternoon."

"Then we shall have them with our tea," Mrs. Tuggle

said. And she turned on the lamp in the parlor.

The light fell on the old woman's face, and goose bumps rose up on Lynn's arms. It was a strange face, but Lynn didn't know exactly why. That one eye was green and the other gray was, of course, rather odd, but it was more than that. Both eyes were small, and peeked out slyly from dark black brows, though Mrs. Tuggle's hair itself was gray. She was small and thin, her shoulders sticking up through her dress like door-knobs. But there was something powerful about the bones of her face, as though the jaw itself was made of steel. Lynn decided that, fragile as she looked, Mrs. Tuggle was capable of enormous strength.

"Sit you down while I put the kettle on," Mrs. Tuggle said. "Oh, *blueberry* muffins. Your mother knows how fond I am of those!"

She took the platter of muffins and disappeared through the door of the kitchen. When she moved, Lynn noticed, she did it swiftly, unlike most women in their seventies. Quick and strong. The goose bumps spread to her back.

"I don't know what I'm doing here," Mouse declared as soon as they were alone. "If I sit down, you'll probably never see me again. I'll probably evaporate."

"I told Mother we'd be polite," Lynn said. "It won't hurt to stay a few minutes." She sat down on the green velvet sofa and looked around.

17

The parlor had a high ceiling, and the walls were decorated with a pale violet paper on which thorny stems twisted and turned, entwining in tall vertical lines till they reached the top, where each stem ended in a single rose. A yellowed shade covered a lamp on a stand, and all the furniture was a deep brown mahogany, old and somewhat dusty, except for the velvet couch and two chairs. On a small table in one corner stood a few framed photographs, and it was these that caught Lynn's eye. She got up and went over to look at the large one in the center.

It was a photograph of the head and shoulders of a young boy about Stevie's age. He was a pale-looking child, with a lock of dark hair that fell partly across his forehead. His eyes, too, looked dark—not only the pupils but the eye sockets, and he wore a thin chain around his neck with a small medallion in front. On the medallion was a spider design. Lynn was still looking at it when Mrs. Tuggle came back in the room.

"Isn't this a picture of your brother, Mrs. Tuggle— the one who drowned?"

"That it is, my dear. He was only six when that picture was taken . . . sixteen when he died. A short life for a fine young lad."

"Did he just fall in or was he swimming?"

"I don't know, child. My husband found him floating face down in the creek, like he'd just laid himself down in the water. How it happened we never knew. One day he was here, the next day he was gone. Ah, but let's have our tea now and your mother's muffins."

Lynn put the photograph back down and came over to the tray where three cups were steaming. Mouse sat gripping the arms of her chair as though she were frozen into position. Mrs. Tuggle noticed.

"Here, Marjorie, a little tea will thaw you out," she said, handing Mouse one of the cups. " 'Tis my own special brew, and it's never a night I go to bed without a spot of it first."

The light from the lamp cast tall shadows on the walls as they raised their cups and lowered them again. The dark furniture suddenly seemed even more massive. The brass knobs of the bureau in one corner looked like two bright eyes, and the row of scalloped edging along the bottom resembled teeth, stretched in a wide, straight grin.

Mouse sipped hesitantly, but as the hot steam bathed her face, she began to relax a little, and finally leaned back in her chair, her bony knees protruding from under the bottom of the long orange tee-shirt.

"And what do I hear of the Beasley family?" Mrs. Tuggle inquired directly. "They say that your mother has gone to Ohio, child. Well, that's between the parents and I won't pry, but a girl without a mother to look after her gets lonely, that's sure. Should ever you want for company, come up the hill and sit with an old woman. 'Twould do us both good."

Mouse didn't answer, but sat with eyes half closed, holding the cup to her face.

"That picture of your brother," Lynn began again, eager to find out more. "What kind of medallion is that around his neck, Mrs. Tuggle?"

Did the old woman frown just a bit, she wondered. The one green eye and the one gray one focused intently on Lynn's face, and it was a moment before the old woman answered.

" 'Tis of no importance, Lynn. We came from Castletown, you know, on the Isle of Man. Wee ones were often given charms to wear—the fashion then, that's all. Sort of to keep the bogles away, you know. Marjorie, dear, hand me that music box on the table—aye, that's the one. 'Twas his favorite toy, this was." Mrs. Tuggle put down her cup and held the small wood box on her lap. With one skinny hand she wound the handle at the side, her lips smiling just a little. It was a strange sort of tune, starting out happy enough but ending on a minor note, and the motion of Mrs. Tuggle's arm made a whirling shadow against the rose stems on the wallpaper.

Something brushed against the back of Lynn's neck. She sprang forward, dropping her muffin on the floor and whirled around. There was the largest cat she had ever seen, slinking along the back of the couch. Mouse turned, but her glasses had steamed up, and when she rubbed her sleeve across them and the cat came into view, she yelped in fright.

" 'Tis only Cat," said Mrs. Tuggle. "He likes the music box. Sits in my lap sometimes, he does, when I play it. Soothes his temper, I suppose."

It looked almost like a raccoon because its fur was so thick—a deep, brown-black in color with no spots or stripes at all, and the slits of its eyes flashed yellow in the light of the lamp.

"A big thing like that ought to be in a zoo!" Mouse declared. "Where did it come from?"

"That I can't say," Mrs. Tuggle replied. "Heard a scratching noise at the door one night, I did, and when I opened it, he walked in. He's been with me ever since."

"He must belong to somebody," Lynn ventured.

"Many a time I've opened the door for him to let him go, but he prowls about the yard a bit and comes back. No, he's a stray, all right, and he's found himself a home. Glad I am to have him, too, for an empty house is a lonely one."

She began winding the music box again. The cat, which had sprung to the top of the old bureau, sat purring loudly, and it seemed to Lynn that she could feel the vibration through the arms of her chair. Then

Mrs. Tuggle began to sing, and her gold tooth, like the cat's yellow eyes, glistened occasionally:

> "Sing of morning, sing of noon,
> Sing of evening's silver moon.
> Feel the darkness, touch the black,
> Hear the shadows whisper back. . . ."

At first Lynn was interested in watching Mrs. Tuggle —the way her eyes fixed themselves on the music box, the way her thin fingers grasped the handle. Then it was the cat that caught her eye. It crouched there behind the old woman, its tail swishing violently, its

eyes looking straight at Lynn, as though reading her thoughts. But suddenly the room seemed far too quiet, and Lynn turned quickly to Mouse to see if she was still there.

Marjorie sat on the chair, her empty teacup in her lap. Her eyelids drooped.

"Mouse," Lynn said. "Listen, I think we'd better go."

Marjorie did not reply, and Lynn was alarmed that something might have happened to her. She reached over and shook her arm. "Mouse, we've got to go."

Suddenly Marjorie's eyes snapped wide open. She looked about, confused.

"You said you had all sorts of things to do tonight,

Mouse," Lynn urged. "I told Mother we wouldn't be long."

Mrs. Tuggle put the music box aside. "Well, another time, then. Come by and see us, Cat and I. And Marjorie, my dear, when you feel you've need of a mother, come to me, child."

She walked to the front door with them. "Truly it's dark now. Be careful of the loose bricks there in the walk. And thank your mother for me, Lynn."

The girls didn't talk till they'd reached the sidewalk in front.

"You were hypnotized, Mouse, I swear it!" Lynn began.

"I wasn't! I knew everything that was going on."

"Well, you sure didn't look like it. You were sitting there with your head tipping to one side. I was really worried! Maybe it was the tea."

Marjorie was quiet for a moment. "I don't think I should ever go back there, Lynn," she said finally. "I really don't. And yet . . . I'm sure I will."

"Mouse, what's happened to you?"

"I don't know. I just can't seem to help myself."

Suddenly, from out of the darkness, came the cackling of a flock of crows. It seemed to come from the direction of the barn behind Mrs. Tuggle's house, but the noise of the cawing got louder till it was directly over the girls' heads.

Lynn and Marjorie stopped and stared upwards. The big black birds could be seen circling around above, and the din of their raucous calling became deafening.

Mouse covered her ears and started to run, Lynn following close behind. Down the brick sidewalk they rushed, past the stone walls and hedges and lampposts till they reached the Morley steps, and the cackling echoed away at last, like laughter against the night sky.

chapter two

"Have you seen Mrs. Tuggle's cat?"

Mrs. Morley sliced Lynn's cream cheese and raisin sandwich in half, stuck it in a plastic bag, and placed it in her lunch sack. She had her jacket on and was ready to leave for the studio. But she always waited till her three children were off to school.

Lynn licked the cinnamon off her toast and watched her mother. "Yes," she said finally. "I saw it when Mouse and I took the muffins up."

"Isn't it huge? It looks like a Persian. It comes to the studio sometimes in the mornings if the air's cold and I have the stove going. It likes to stretch out on the floor where it's warm. Cats don't live very exciting lives, do they?"

This time Lynn didn't answer. She ran her finger over the plate to get the last of the sugar, finished her orange juice, winced at the sour taste, and went up to brush her teeth.

A blast of rock music trailed past the bathroom door and on downstairs as Judith and her transistor radio went by, then sounded again as Judith came back up.

"Lynn," she said from the doorway, "can't you do anything about Marjorie? I saw her in the drugstore the other day, and it looked as if she was wearing one of her father's shirts and not much else. I mean, she doesn't actually go to school dressed like that, does she?"

Lynn sloshed the water around in her mouth and spit it out. The first week Mouse had come to school one day in her pajama tops and jeans and once during the second week she had worn a jogging outfit, but Lynn couldn't remember Marjorie wearing her father's shirts to school. Socks, maybe, but not shirts.

"I don't understand why you get upset about it," Lynn said. "She's not in your school. You don't have to look at her."

"Just thinking about her makes me upset," Judith said. "I keep thinking how everyone's going to laugh and make fun of her when she gets to junior high, and if *you* can't get her to take better care of herself, it's hopeless. I mean, now that her mother's in Ohio, we've got to sort of look out for her, you know?"

"Sure," Lynn said, wondering.

"Good." The music grew fainter as Judith went downstairs again, and this time she went out and shut the door.

Lynn looked in the mirror and tried pinning her pony tail on top of her head, but it fell down on each side around her ears, so she gave up. She wished she had Judith's long black hair and Judith's large brown eyes set in that China-doll face. So Judith was actually concerned about Mouse—self-centered old Judith! Maybe she really was maturing after all, like Mother said she would once she reached the ninth grade.

When Lynn went downstairs, Mrs. Morley was pinning a piece of paper to Stevie's shirt with his name and address in large print.

"How long does he have to wear that?" Lynn asked.

"This is the last day. School requirements. Too many kindergarten children take the wrong turn and end up lost, so they have to wear address tags for the first three weeks."

"Well, it's dumb," said Stevie disgustedly.

Mrs. Morley kissed him. "I want you back safe and sound," she said. "Come on and I'll walk as far as the corner with you."

"Have a good day, Stevie," Lynn said. "I'll be along later. I'm waiting for Mouse."

When the door closed the second time, Lynn went

upstairs to get her gym clothes ready. Her room was on the third floor. In fact, it *was* the third floor—hers and Judith's—and a heavy curtain in the middle separated one girl's territory from the other's. Lynn folded her gym suit and socks into a neat bundle and put them in her schoolbag along with her lunch and sweater. She could hear Mother singing outside on the sidewalk, and occasionally Stevie's little voice chimed in.

The Morley household was cheerful and relaxed when Mother was working on the second draft of a book—even better, however, when she was writing the third. The first was the most difficult, she always said. It was the skeleton of the story, the laborious fitting together of all the bones on paper. It was long and tedious, and it was during this period that Lynn could never understand why Mother wanted to write in the first place, for it made her cross and irritable.

The second draft was the flesh and blood, Mother said, and took only half as long to do. The plot would begin to shape up, the characters to stir, the suspense to build, and Mrs. Morley's spirits rose along with it. This was where Mother was now. It was during third drafts, however, that Lynn realized what writing meant to her mother and why she would never be happy doing anything else. The third draft was the soul, when the whole story came alive.

Happy birthday, Sylvia, Dad had scribbled once on a card that went with her present. *May all your birthdays be third drafts.*

Glancing out the window, she saw Mouse coming up the street. She threw her schoolbag over her shoulder, clattering downstairs to second, another flight to the landing, and another flight to first. Closing the door behind her, she went down the steps to the walk, then down a steeper flight to the main sidewalk where Mouse was waiting.

This time Marjorie's clothes were even worse than Judith could have imagined. She had on an old paint-stained sweat shirt over a pair of Bermuda shorts. As usual, her socks didn't match, and one sneaker had no laces at all.

Lynn thought about it as they walked up the hill and made the turn. There was something more to all this than casualness. It seemed more like a deliberate attempt to look awful. Mouse had never cared very much about clothes, it was true, but since her mother had moved away, Mouse's appearance had gone from bad to worse.

"Sort of chilly for shorts, isn't it?" Lynn commented finally.

Mouse shrugged. "Sun's hot. It'll warm up later. Listen, Lynn, I think I understand about Mrs. Tuggle's cat. It's her familiar."

"Her familiar? What kind of English is that? You mean it looks familiar?"

"No, I mean it *is* her familiar. All witches have one. I was reading about it last night. It's a demon that stays around a witch to help her out, and it's usually in the form of an animal, like a goat or cat or bird or lizard."

"What book were you reading?"

"*Spells and Potions*—that rare book that Daddy bought for his shop."

Lynn thought it over. "Mrs. Tuggle says that the cat just came to her one night—scratched at the door and she let it in."

"More likely she conjured it up," Mouse said. "It could even be the soul of a dead person, bodily transfigured into the form of a cat. Witches can do that too, you know."

They reached the school and jostled their way through the groups of students in the hall till they came to their room at the end. Two girls standing by the window stared at Mouse, then turned away, giggling. Lynn pretended she hadn't noticed, but inside, she was hurting for her friend.

Mouse slid into her seat and slouched down till her feet were under the seat in front of her. A boy in the next row reached over and tapped her on the shoulder.

"Hey, where's your paint bucket?" he teased.

Mouse didn't answer. She pulled up the big glasses that always slid down her nose, took out her geography book, and seemed absorbed in the first chapter.

But Lynn, watching from across the room, knew that Mouse wasn't reading at all. And in spite of acting so cool and nonchalant, she knew that Mouse was miserable. Was it possible Lynn wondered, that Marjorie felt her mother didn't care for her, which probably wasn't true at all? And if her own mother didn't care, then how could anyone else? And if nobody cared, why should she care about herself? In fact, if she looked awful enough, maybe somebody would pay attention.

Lynn had known Mouse for a long time. Nobody had ever been such a good friend. Marjorie had always been there to help when Lynn needed her. And now that Mouse needed somebody, Lynn wanted to help, but she wasn't sure how.

As usual, when the girls had something on their minds, they talked it over at their secret place in the old cemetery. When school let out at three, they walked back to Water Street, crossed over, and made their way down the steep hill to the creek, then up the bank on the other side until they reached the spiked fence. The high iron gate that had long since rusted open swung creakily on its upper hinge. Tall grass grew up around the gravestones, and the entire place was com-

32

pletely silent except for the rustle of wind in the branches above. Somewhere down by Cowden's Creek one crow cawed, then another.

Lynn and Marjorie walked slowly, parting the high grass as they walked, till they came to the half-dead oak tree. There the tombstone of Mrs. Elfreda Lewis had long since fallen down in front of the tombstone of Mr. Lewis, making a perfect high-backed chair. This was Lynn's seat. Mouse sat across from her on a marble scroll held between two angels, the grave of C. L. Pritchard, and draped an arm around each angel's neck. Her eyebrows frowned behind the big circles of her glasses. Finally she said, "I think Mrs. Tuggle is trying to form a coven of witches, like the book said. Each additional witch raises the cone of power. The more girls she can get, the more she can do. She chooses them one at a time."

"And one of us is next, Mouse. I know it," Lynn added. "All last summer she tried to get Judith. Then Judith got sick and lost interest in going to Mrs. Tuggle's house any more. In fact, she almost lost her memory. She hardly ever talks about her now, and she used to go up there every night."

They were quiet a moment, trying to fit the pieces together.

"If we . . . we ever gave in, Lynn," Mouse said finally, ". . . I mean, if we ever went to her house and let her teach us witchcraft, we would never be the same again. I'm sure of it."

Lynn paled. Mouse was the authority on witches, and she must know what she was talking about. If she only knew how close Lynn had come to having her feelings swept away. In spite of all her fears and distrust and horror of Mrs. Tuggle, in spite of the sense of evil, there was also a deep curiosity inside herself, and this, she saw now, was the most dangerous thing of all. What *would* it be like to be involved in witchcraft—to have that power over people and the things that happened to them? The attraction was there, whether she liked it or not. And it might draw her in against her will.

"How would we be different, Mouse?"

"We wouldn't have control over ourselves any longer; we would be in the power of witchcraft. We might not even be friends—not like we are now, anyway. All that would matter to us would be Mrs. Tuggle and what she wanted us to do."

"Glory, Mouse! How can we be sure we're not trapped already?"

"Because Daddy's rare book said that before you can be drawn into witchcraft, you have to want it more than anything else at some particular moment. As long as you always want something else more, it can't take you. As long as we want to be friends more than we want to be witches, she can't hurt us."

Still Lynn had doubts. "But what if . . . for just a tiny fraction of a minute . . . we were just sort of overcome with curiosity?"

"I don't know." Mouse looked grave. "If Mrs. Tuggle wasn't around, I suppose we'd be okay. But if we felt that way for even a fraction of a minute when she was using her full power on us, then nothing could save us."

The air was so still that Lynn could hear herself breathing. Did she dare trust herself to go to Mrs. Tuggle's again? And what about Mouse? Marjorie was the one who was most suggestible. She took a deep breath.

"So Mrs. Tuggle, for some reason, wants to build up a coven. Is that all a witch has to do to get her full powers?"

"No," Mouse said. "There's something else. Maybe she's already done it."

"What?"

"Murder a younger brother or sister."

Lynn stared at Mouse. "C. L. Pritchard. Who else?"

Mouse unwrapped her arms from around the angels' necks and tapped thoughtfully on the tombstone beneath her. "How long would it take to dig up a grave, Lynn?"

"Uh-uh. That's out. The body's been buried, Mouse, for forty years! How could we prove he'd been murdered? And besides, there's a law against it. You'd have to have a court order. You have to have a court order for everything."

Again they were silent. The cemetery was a good talking place because they were alone, and yet Lynn often had the feeling that someone else was around. It was as though the tall trees themselves were listening.

"Oh, Mouse!" she said suddenly.

"What?"

"If I *did* fall under Mrs. Tuggle's spell, and if she *did* make me a witch, and *I* wanted to obtain *my* full powers. . . ."

They stared at each other.

"That's right," Mouse whispered. "You'd have to murder Stevie."

Lynn gulped. "She *couldn't* get me," she declared firmly. "She *couldn't!* I just would never let it happen!" She sat thinking, and then turned slowly to her friend. "Mouse, how strong are you?"

"Seventy-eight pounds."

"No. I mean psychologically. If Mrs. Tuggle were to use all her powers, could you hold out against her?"

"I'd buckle right under, Lynn, beginning at the knees."

"That's what I was afraid of. Then we've got to keep you away from her. If you don't have anything to do with her at all, I don't see how she can hurt you. But I've got to find out more somehow. There must be evidence around, if we just knew where to look."

Marjorie's eyes were still frowning. "So if she murdered her brother forty years ago to become a full power witch, what's she been doing all this time? How come she's just now getting around to form a coven?"

"I've wondered about that too. Of course, we *don't* know exactly what she's been doing all these years. Maybe she's been working on it all along."

Suddenly Mouse sat up. "Lynn, when did she first ask Judith to come over and sew?"

"Sometime last winter. February, maybe."

"And when did the town first start talking about digging up the old cemetery?"

"Good grief, Mouse. How should I know?" Lynn thought for a moment. "Didn't it first make the newspaper after the town meeting in January?"

"Right."

"So?"

"So there's some reason she doesn't want anyone to dig up the old cemetery. Maybe she needs all the power she can get to stop it."

"Mouse, you're brilliant! You really are!" Lynn stared at her admiringly, and suddenly she thought it was the appropriate time to add something else. "Now if you just *looked* brilliant, you'd really be something! Look, Mouse, do me a favor and don't wear that sweat shirt to school again."

37

Marjorie seemed a little embarrassed. "Heck, I don't care how I look," she said.

"*I* care about you, Mouse," Lynn said earnestly.

Mouse stood up and dug the toe of her sneaker in the grass. "If it embarrasses you to be seen with me—"

"It's not that, Mouse. If it made you happy, I wouldn't care, but I don't think it does. If it really made you happy, I wouldn't care if you came to school naked." And then, because she wasn't too sure of what Mouse would do next she said, "Erase, erase. I didn't mean it. But I *do* care, Mouse, really, because I like you more than anyone else."

They both started down the hill to the creek again, which separated them from the hill on the other side, the meadow, and the houses up along the rim. It was odd, but there seemed to be something different about the water in the creek as it passed behind Mrs. Tuggle's house. Lynn had noticed it before, but it had made little impression on her until now. Cowden's Creek was wide, four feet deep in places, and good for swimming. For the most part it flowed slowly in a lazy kind of current. If you dropped a stick in the water near the cemetery, it took forever, it seemed, to get down to the business district. But the part of the creek that ran behind Mrs. Tuggle's meadow was different. Here the water was deepest, and seemed to flow in several directions at once, perhaps because of the huge rocks that dotted the creek bottom. But there was something more. Sometimes, when Lynn looked down in the water here, it was as though her reflection were changing, and the little whirlpools that appeared here and there were sucking in her very soul. There were even certain times of the year when a sort of steaming mist seemed to rise up from this part of the creek and nowhere else.

Lynn started to tell Mouse about it when all at once she felt a tug on her arm and then she was yanked down hard in the tall grass. Mouse crouched beside her, one finger to her lips.

From somewhere on the other side of the bank came the soft crackling sound of footsteps in the underbrush; and when Lynn raised her head and peered through the weeds, she could make out Mrs. Tuggle on the opposite side, walking with her back toward them.

But it wasn't just the crunch of grass that broke the stillness. From the trees overhead came the loud cawing of crows, cackling in concert. The girls waited.

The old woman stopped and stretched out her arms.

"Bathim, Pursan, Abigar," she chanted. "Shaddar, Asmon, Loray; Valefar, Marbos, Pruslos. . . ."

Instantly the crows came flying down, nine in all, and landed on Mrs. Tuggle's outstretched arms.

"Mouse!" Lynn whispered in terror.

Marjorie was shaking so violently that her arms vibrated against Lynn's.

Mrs. Tuggle's gray hair, usually done up in a tight bun, hung loose around her shoulders, and blew in thin wisps as the wind caught it. Soft animallike noises came from her throat, cooing sounds, guttural grunts, as she talked first to the birds on her left and then on her right.

All at once she lifted her arms quickly toward the sky, and the crows flew off, cawing loudly, and roosted in the tall sycamore there on the bank. Mrs. Tuggle took a few steps toward her house on the hill, then stopped. She stood absolutely motionless, like a fox sniffing the air. Then suddenly she turned and looked directly at the place where the girls were hiding, smiled, and went on up the hill.

"Oh, lordie, Lynn, did she see us?" Mouse bleated, and her voice shook with every syllable. "Did she know we were here?"

"She always knows," said Lynn.

They got up, walking along the creek in the other direction till they came to the swinging footbridge that connected both banks, and crossed over.

"I'm not going home," Mouse said suddenly. "If anything jumped out at me—a cricket, even—I'd faint. I'm going to walk into town and stay at Daddy's store till he closes." She followed the creek on down toward the business district, and Lynn went up through the meadow to her house, her heart still pounding.

When she reached Mother's garden, she paused for

just a moment and looked back. Mouse was growing smaller and smaller as she tramped through the weeds by the creek. She looked so tiny and weak and vulnerable, somehow—dwarfed by the tall trees that rose up here and there along the bank. And then Lynn's heart almost stopped beating, for nine black crows were moving swiftly from one treetop to the next, following Mouse.

As the days went on, it became clear to Lynn just whom it was that Mrs. Tuggle was after, for the crows followed Marjorie wherever she went. They did not come down and fly about her head, making it obvious. In fact, Mouse herself had not noticed. But they were always there, in a tree nearby, and there were always nine. Marjorie was the weakest of the two girls, and Mrs. Tuggle knew it. The old woman had made her choice.

For five days Lynn said nothing, not even to Mouse. Marjorie had enough problems without worrying about nine black shadows overhead who were always watching, always waiting. But Lynn observed how they followed Mouse to school each day and home again— quiet, seldom cawing or attracting attention to themselves; and whenever she counted, the number was always the same. Nine. What did it mean?

Lynn decided to hold a conference with herself.

She had done it once when she wasn't getting along well with a teacher at school and felt she'd been treated unfairly. She did it another time when she decided she was wasting her allowance. Now it was time for still another conference, and this one, she knew, was the most serious of all because it involved her best friend.

On a Thursday afternoon when Mother and Stevie had gone to the post office, Lynn went up to her bedroom on the third floor and lay down, staring up at the slanted ceiling. She tried to think of nothing at all, to rid her mind of clutter. She liked to think of herself during these sessions as both the psychiatrist and the patient, and proceeded to ask herself questions out loud. It was essential that she be absolutely honest in her answer:

"How long have you felt that Mrs. Tuggle was a witch?"

"Since spring, after Judith had been going to her house for several months and began acting strangely."

"What proof did you really find that they were practicing witchcraft?"

"None—just a lot of things going on that seemed strange, that hadn't happened before. But Mom and Dad called them 'coincidences'."

"And now that Judith isn't going to Mrs. Tuggle's anymore, and seems to have forgotten the whole thing, why can't you let it drop?"

"Because I'm afraid for Mouse."

"*There must be more to it than that. Mouse could stay away from her if she's so scared. You know that if you stayed away, Mouse would too. You're the one who dragged her up there the other night.*"

"But the crows. . . ."

"*Isn't it true that you're really very curious about Mrs. Tuggle, and even if the crows stopped following Marjorie, you'd still want to find out?*"

"Yes, I suppose I would. There's something about her that draws me to her and that scares me. I'm afraid to go without somebody along."

"*Then you're more eager to satisfy your curiosity than you are to protect Mouse?*"

"That's the way it seems, doesn't it? Okay, I'll never take Mouse up there again."

"*It's not your worry anyway. If Mrs. Tuggle really is a witch, it will come out eventually, and the adults will take care of it.*"

"But I can't get her out of my mind. I have this terrible feeling of evil when I'm near her. And it's impossible to stay away completely, with Mother renting her hen house and asking me to run errands and things."

"*A feeling of evil is not exactly proof of evil. She's kept to herself for a long time and is bound to seem strange. If you help spread rumors about her, you make it hard for anybody to see her as anything other than a witch.*"

"I know that, and sometimes I worry about it. But I don't think I'm the kind of person who spreads rumors. One time in school everybody thought Jonathan Kelly was stealing things from people's desks. I never even liked him, but I said we shouldn't be talking about him till somebody had proof. And when it turned out that it really *was* somebody else, I was glad for Jonathan."

"But isn't there a little bit of excitement in all of this for you? Maybe you don't really want to hurt Mrs. Tuggle or ruin her reputation, but you enjoy the suspense."

"At first I think that was true. When the feeling started last spring, it was just a suspicion that grew—a hunch. But now I think I'm more afraid than I am excited. I don't want it to go any further. I want the whole thing to stop. If I wanted excitement, I would have told Mouse right away about the crows following her, and everybody else at school, too. Think what excitement that would cause! I could have the whole class stirred up! I could arrange nightly expeditions up to Mrs. Tuggle's house and appoint lookouts all around and hold secret meetings and everything. If it was just a game, that's what I'd do. But it's not."

"Yet surely, you can't really believe in witchcraft."

"I know that when strange things happen that no one can explain, it doesn't automatically mean that witches are responsible. But it doesn't mean they *aren't* responsible, either. . . ."

There were footsteps on the stairs, and Judith came in. Because the doorway to the third floor was on Lynn's side of the curtain, she had to pass through Lynn's section of the attic bedroom before she could get to her own.

"Who were you talking to?" she asked, as she pulled the curtain aside and went over to her dresser.

"Myself."

"Uh-oh. That's the first sign of going loony, you know." Judith took out a red scarf and tied back her long dark hair. "What are you lying around up here for anyway? It's a gorgeous afternoon. The trees down by the creek are beginning to change. If you stand out on the back porch you can see them. I couldn't wait for school to get out so I could go hiking."

Lynn rolled over on her side and propped her head up with one hand. "Judith, what did you used to do at Mrs. Tuggle's?"

"Sew. Why?"

"I know, but you would stay there all evening. What did you talk about all that time?"

Judith stood in front of the mirror a moment longer, fussing with the scarf. Finally she turned and looked at Lynn. "You know, I just can't remember. That's funny, isn't it? Everytime I try to think, it gets all mixed up with dreams I've had till I don't know which was real and which was imagined. A psychological block, that's it."

Lynn got up and went downstairs. She stood out on the back porch, as Judith had suggested, and looked out over the garden, holding the screen door open. Even the meadow beyond was changing color as it stretched off down the hill to the trees below, their leaves glowing red and gold in the afternoon sunlight. Everything seemed so quiet and peaceful, it did seem silly to worry. Mrs. Tuggle had lived in the town since she was a young bride of twenty, having come over from England with her new husband and her little orphaned brother. Lynn had never heard of the old woman harming anybody. Perhaps she was just getting senile and merely fancied herself a witch. Perhaps all the scary stories of the hobyahs and bogles she had been reared on had finally addled her mind, and she really thought she had supernatural powers. Maybe it was merely an old woman's way of trying to make herself more important than she really was. Perhaps it was sheer loneliness. . . . The trees were the same, changing color year after year; the houses were the same, the old brick sidewalks. . . . If Mrs. Tuggle hadn't done anyone harm yet, she probably wouldn't now. Yet, those crows. . . .

Something moved in the bushes below. Lynn looked down but saw nothing. Just an undulation of leaves, like the motion in tall grass when a snake wriggles through it. But suddenly a dark object leaped out and dashed up the steps. Mrs. Tuggle's cat leaped to the table along one wall of the porch. It stood for a moment with its tail swishing, its yellow eyes flashing, and then began a slow walk along the table, one paw in front of the other, watching Lynn. When it reached the edge, it turned and started back the other way, like a panther in a cage.

There was a flash of something shiny in the cat's fur, something Lynn had not noticed the first time she met the animal. She took a step closer. The cat stopped, watching her come. Something hung about its neck, a collar perhaps. Lynn stretched out her hand. The cat waited. Slowly Lynn's fingers searched the thick fur under the cat's chin, till they touched a silver chain. Running her fingers along it, she felt a small hanging object, and when she lifted it up, she saw that it was engraved with a spider mark on one side.

chapter three

Lynn did not have long to wonder whether she should
tell Mouse about either the crows or the spider medallion, because the phone rang just then and a terrified
voice pleaded, "Lynn, come over quick!"

"What's wrong, Mouse? What's happened?"

"Oh, hurry! I'll tell you later."

Lynn dropped the receiver back on the phone and
bounded out the front door. Rushing down the porch
steps, she crossed the lawn, jumped off the rock wall
to the brick sidewalk below, and ran down the hill two
blocks to the Beasley home. She could see Marjorie
waiting for her behind the screen. As soon as Lynn
came up on the porch, Mouse stepped out. Her eyes

were huge behind the heavy lens of her round glasses, but the rest of her small face looked pinched and drained of color.

"Look up there," she said, pointing to a large walnut tree by her house.

Lynn looked up, already knowing. There were the nine black crows, silent, watching.

"I think they've been following me," Mouse whispered in a tense, dry voice. "I noticed them on my way to school this morning, but I didn't think much about it. Then, after I left you at your house coming home, I noticed they followed me along, from tree to tree. When I went to the drugstore just now, I watched to see what they would do. They followed me all the way there, and were waiting for me when I came out. Oh, Lynn!" She threw her arms around her friend. "I'm so scared. What are they going to do to me?"

Lynn could feel her shaking. "Mouse, I don't know! I didn't want to scare you, but I noticed the crows following you a week ago when we saw Mrs. Tuggle that day by the creek. After I got up the hill, I looked back and saw them. I didn't know what to do! I knew you'd be scared silly if I told you."

They clung to each other for another moment, and suddenly Lynn pushed away, grabbing Mouse by the shoulders. "It's even worse than that, though. I've got to tell you something else."

"Oh, lordie, Lynn. I don't think I want to know."

"Okay. I guess I'd better not."

"No, no! I've got to find out. Oh, Lynn, I think I'm going to die I'm so frightened. Tell me quick and get it over with."

"Well, this afternoon I was standing out on the back porch and suddenly Mrs. Tuggle's cat ran up the steps and leaped up on the table where we keep the geraniums. I saw something gleaming around the cat's neck, so I looked, and—"

"You touched it?" Mouse shrieked. "You touched the cat?"

"Yes—"

"Oh, Lynn, you shouldn't have done that! I read about that in the book. It gives the animal power over you. . . ."

Lynn sat down on the steps so her knees wouldn't buckle underneath her. Marjorie crouched beside her.

"Did you pet it? Stroke it?"

"No. But my fingers touched the fur when I reached for the chain."

"What chain?"

"It had a silver chain around its neck. And Mouse, there's a medallion on the end, with a spider mark on it! It's the same one I saw in the photograph of Mrs. Tuggle's brother. He was wearing it around his neck."

Mouse sat with one hand over her mouth, eyes huge.

"Is it possible, Lynn?" she breathed at last. "Do you think it could really happen that her brother has come back in the form of a cat?"

"I don't know what to think, Mouse. Can you imagine anyone believing that? No one would listen in a million years."

"No. But the crows. . . ."

"They'll believe *that!*" Lynn said suddenly, jumping up. "They'll *have* to. They can see it with their own eyes. Come on, Mouse. We're going down to your father's store and show him."

They started down the street to the business district, their eyes on the trees overhead. With a shrill cry to the others, the lead crow, the largest of the nine, flapped his wings and rose up in the air, moving on to the next tree and the others followed . . . down to Lindon's Corner, then three blocks on Main, past the shoe repair shop, the beauty parlor, the delicatessen, and finally Mr. Beasley's bookstore. The crows lit on the roof of the library across the street.

The girls, unsmiling and frightened, went inside. Mr. Beasley was ringing up a sale and chatting with a man by the cash register.

"Hello, girls," he said and went on talking. But something about Marjorie's face made him turn and look at her again, and soon he cut his conversation short and opened the door for the customer.

With the store empty again, he turned to his daughter. "You sick, Marjorie? Stomach upset or something?"

Mouse shook her head, but her lips trembled and the glasses bobbed off her nose at an angle as she wiped her eyes. "Daddy, there are birds following m . . . me," she stammered, and somehow Lynn wished she'd put it differently.

"There are what?"

"Crows," Lynn said quickly. "I've known it for a week, Mr. Beasley, but I didn't want to upset her."

"But today I noticed them following me to school, and when I went to the drugstore, they followed me there and back, and now they followed me all the way down here," Mouse added breathlessly.

"Since when were you ever afraid of crows?" her father smiled. "This is crow country, girl . . . the great Midwest. There are always flocks around in the fall."

"But this is different, Daddy! They've been following me and nobody else. Everywhere I go they fly in the treetops."

"And there are always nine," Lynn said. "I've been counting them, the same nine crows, and they have a leader."

Mr. Beasley frowned and looked rather severely at Lynn. "And how do you know they're the same nine? Can you honestly tell one crow from another?"

"You can see them, Mr. Beasley. You can watch them yourself. No matter where Marjorie goes, they go along and wait for her."

Mr. Beasley turned back to the door, opened it, and stepped outside, looking up at the sky. "Okay," he said. "Where are they?"

"Right over there. . . ." Mouse said, pointing to the library, but her voice trailed off because the roof was bare. There were no crows in sight.

Lynn and Mouse turned around and around on the sidewalk, looking up at the roof tops and window ledges. But there wasn't a bird anywhere.

"Marjorie, I haven't got time for this kind of game," Mr. Beasley grumbled, opening the door again.

"But they were there, Daddy! They were! Just a moment ago!"

Marjorie's father turned to Lynn. "And you, young lady, have got an imagination that's going to get you in trouble some day. You're a great girl, Lynn, but sometimes you really get Marjorie hooked on something—witches and sorcerers and I don't know what all, and I think we ought to call a halt to it right now. You're both creative kids, and you can think of something better to do with your time than scare each other to death."

He stepped inside the door, then put his head back out, looking grumpy:

"Marjorie, there's a meat loaf in the refrigerator. Stick it in the oven with a couple of potatoes around five-thirty, and I'll try to be home by dinnertime."

Silently Lynn and Mouse walked across the street and sat down on a bench, embarrassed at the scene on the sidewalk. There seemed to be nothing to say. How could they possibly fight Mrs. Tuggle and all her tricks? At that moment they noticed the cat sitting on the steps of the library, a strange animal smile on its face. And then, from the direction of Cowden's Creek, came the nine crows, one by one, alighting there on the roof.

Lynn looked across the street to the bookshop to see if by some miracle Mr. Beasley might look out and see them. But he was working on the shelves along the far wall and had his back to the door.

There was no point in talking to her own father about it, Lynn knew. He was having his own problems. The town was divided between people who wanted the community to stay just as it had always been and people who wanted to replace old things with new.

"The answer lies somewhere in between," Mr. Morley said one Saturday after he had still another call from citizens worried about what was going to happen. "Some people only want what's good for business and never think at all about beauty or the character and personality of a town. And some people are so hung up on keeping things the way they are that they can't understand that some changes might really be for the best."

"Have they made a decision about the cemetery?" Mother asked from the easy chair where she sat with her manuscript in her lap.

"No. We're still trying to locate all the relatives of people buried there to see if they would give permission to move the graves to the new cemetery on the east side. A lot of people have grumbled that no one keeps up the old cemetery anyway because it's never been clear who is legally responsible. Frankly, it's a mess, and I don't think we're going to reach a decision any time soon."

"Has anyone called on Mrs. Tuggle yet about moving her brother's grave?"

Lynn, who was working on a history paper, stopped writing and listened.

"No, and it gets stranger every day. I sent one of the clerks over to the library to look up microfilms of forty-year-old newspapers. He can't find a single mention of a boy named Pritchard drowning—no story— nothing. And the death certificate still hasn't turned up."

"But you *know* it's Mrs. Tuggle's brother. Everybody knows it. She says so herself. Why do you need anything else?"

"I don't really. But once the secretaries got started

talking, I thought it would help to get the original story and stop all the gossip that's going around. But there's not even an obituary. It's really weird. One of the women in payroll said that her mother told her there was never any funeral, either—that Mrs. Tuggle just began telling people that the boy had drowned, and a new gravestone went up in the cemetery."

"Then you *do* believe there might be something to all the gossip," said Lynn.

Mrs. Morley glanced at her. "Little pitchers have big ears," she murmured.

"I don't believe anything of the kind, Lynn," Father said. "Years ago the courthouse wasn't so systematic about keeping records. Anything could have happened, and a funeral ceremony isn't necessary, you know. A body has to be buried, but there's nothing on the books that says there has to be a service. Just because we can't find any story or death certificate doesn't mean that someone was murdered."

"Who was murdered?" piped up Stevie from the dining room where he was drawing helicopters on long sheets of shelf paper. He jumped off his chair and stood in the doorway. "Who was murdered, Daddy?"

"See?" said Mr. Morley to Lynn. "That's exactly the way rumors get started. That's the way it was at the courthouse. One of the secretaries made an offhand remark—wondered about something out loud—and someone else picked it up, embellished it a little and passed it on, and the first thing we know there's a murderess at large."

"*Who?*" Steve demanded.

"Nobody," said Father, emphatically. "A figment of the imagination, that's what."

"A what?" said Stevie, confused. And then he got angry. "Nobody ever tells me anything! You've always got secrets!" He threw down his pencil and buried his head in one arm, leaning against the doorway. "Just because I'm little, nobody ever tells me secrets!" he bellowed.

Mrs. Morley put her manuscript aside. "Come here, Stevie, and I'll tell you a secret, just for you," she coaxed.

Stevie sauntered over, his lower lip sticking out, and stood grumpily by her chair. She pulled him down to whisper in his ear, but Lynn, sitting only a few feet away, could hear. "We're having liver for supper, and afterwards I'm going to let you take a little bit up to Mrs. Tuggle's and feed it to her cat."

"I've got a secret about liver!" Stevie yelped importantly, marching around the living room.

Lynn watched her father tie his work shoes and go outside to put on the storm windows. Stevie tagged along to help, leaving Lynn and her mother in the quiet of the living room. Mrs. Morley picked up her manuscript again and chewed on the stem of her glasses while she read over the last paragraph.

"How's the book coming, Mother?" Lynn asked.

"Well, better than it was, but there's still a long way to go before it comes alive. Sometimes I think my writing lacks variety. There are too many pages of narrative. Not enough dialogue to keep it moving."

"I know a song—a poem, sort of. You could put it in the book. You could have one of the witches sing it, maybe."

Mother smiled. "Let's hear it."

Lynn didn't know how the melody went, but she remembered the words:

> *"Sing of morning, sing of noon,*
> *Sing of evening's silver moon.*
> *Feel the darkness, touch the black,*
> *Hear the shadows whisper back."*

"Why, that's lovely, Lynn. It's both eerie and lilting. I wonder if it's copyrighted. Where did you see it?"

"I didn't. Mrs. Tuggle sang it the evening Marjorie and I took her the muffins."

"Doesn't she have some interesting songs, though? You have a good memory for words, Lynn. Maybe you'll want to do some sort of writing yourself some day—"

"No," Lynn declared. "I'm going to be a psychiatrist."

60

"A psychiatrist?" Mrs. Morley leaned back and gave Lynn her full attention. "Well, that would be an interesting profession. What made you think of that?"

"Because I'm interested in people. I like to know what they're thinking—why they do what they do. I mean, well . . . take Mouse. The way she dresses, the way she's been acting since her mother moved away. Why do some people care how they look, and others don't? Why are some people selfish, and others aren't? Why are some people afraid of snakes and things, and other people pick them right up? I just like to know things like that."

"But being a psychiatrist is a lot more than just knowing things. It's helping people feel better about themselves."

"I know. And I wish I could do that for Mouse."

"It's got to come from inside, honey—the feeling that she's worth something to somebody. But you can do a lot by showing her you're her friend no matter what. She needs a lot of extra love these days. Mrs. Tuggle and I were talking about it the other morning—how sad it is—a girl her age without a mother close by—"

"Mother, I wish you wouldn't talk to Mrs. Tuggle about Marjorie."

"But why not? She's concerned."

"It's just that . . . well, Mouse is sensitive about these things, and she wouldn't want everyone talking about her."

"I haven't said anything to anyone that I wouldn't say in front of Marjorie, herself," Mrs. Morley said, "but if you think she would object, I won't discuss her again."

Mother seemed so willing to talk, so understanding, that Lynn was on the verge of telling her about the crows and the charm around the cat's neck. She wanted so much to share her fears with somebody. But she stopped, her lips pressed together. She knew that were she to try to show Mother the crows, they would disappear as before. And as for the charm around the cat's neck, Mrs. Morley did not believe in the significance of such things. No, it would be best to wait for another time. Proof. If only she had proof she could hold in her hand, something that wouldn't fly away.

Mouse, however, had nothing at all against charms. When Lynn met her outside the house Monday on the way to school, she noticed that Marjorie was wearing a tarnished silver ring.

"What's that on your finger?" she asked. The ring was also too big. Mouse had wound adhesive tape around it in back to make it fit more tightly.

"Protection," Mouse said simply. "Lynn, I just had to. I've been so scared." Her eyes darted up to the trees along the street where the crows, of course, were waiting. "I read some more in that book on spells and potions, and found a charm that's supposed to give protection from witches. You have to take the ring of someone who has died, wrap it in silk, bury it under an oak tree for one night, dip it in vinegar, and hold it over the flame of a candle while you repeat seven times,

> Wind and water, earth and sky,
> Keep me safe from witches."

"Is that all?" asked Lynn.

"That's all. But I have to wear it constantly. If I ever take it off, even for a minute, the book said, the power is gone."

"So where did you get the ring, Mouse?" Lynn was almost afraid to ask. When Mouse was desperate, she'd do anything.

"It used to belong to my grandmother, and she's dead. I wrapped it in one of mother's old silk scarves, buried it under the oak tree in our yard on Saturday night, dipped it in vinegar Sunday morning, and recited the words while I held it over a flame with tweezers. But I don't feel any braver. I'll bet it doesn't work."

"Just the same, don't take it off, Mouse. Maybe it's one of those power-of-positive-thinking things. If you really *believe* it will work, you'll actually be braver and more able to protect yourself. Anyway, why don't you bring that book over after school and we'll see if there's anything else in it we could use."

"I can't. It's one of Daddy's rare books. I can't take

it out of the house. He doesn't even know I've been reading it. And we'd better not let him catch us, either, because he'll say you're influencing me again to believe in witchcraft."

"Is that what he really thinks?"

"He said it last night at dinner."

They walked on for a way without talking. It was awful not to be believed, especially by people who loved you and would be concerned if anything happened. It was like the bad dreams that Lynn had from time to time in which something horrible was happening to her. Maybe she was standing in a rowboat and it was drifting out to sea. Or she was sitting in a meadow and a pack of wolves was coming closer and closer. And always, when she would call out to her parents to come and rescue her, they would just look at her and go on talking as though it were nothing at all. Then suddenly they would realize she really was in danger, but it would be too late. At that point Lynn always woke up, her heart pounding, her forehead wet with perspiration, feeling both terrified and angry.

By mid-October, it was obvious to Lynn that the presence of the crows was affecting them both. Lynn and Mouse withdrew to themselves, their voices more subdued, eyes on the trees. The other girls seemed to take the hint and leave them alone. Once, at recess, when the others were jumping rope out on the sidewalk, a fifth-grader pointed to the crows and said she bet they had a nest up there because she'd noticed them sitting there that morning. At that the crows flew away. Mouse and Lynn looked at each other, but said nothing. The birds did not return until it was time to go home, but by then the other girls had forgotten and no longer noticed them at all.

It was the effect on Mouse that worried Lynn the most. Marjorie had always been a good student—B average, at least. And now she found it hard to concentrate on her work. Often Lynn noticed that she read only half the chapter the teacher assigned, or did not turn in any homework at all. She rarely raised her hand in class, but sat staring out the window during group discussions. Once the teacher spoke to her sharply, telling her to keep her thoughts on her work. But then after school she apologized to Mouse and said she knew that things had been sort of difficult for her at home. Another time, during a social studies test, a large crow flew right down on the window ledge by Marjorie's seat, and Mouse burst into tears. The teacher sent her to the health room to lie down.

Slowly Lynn was coming to a decision. She could not let it go on any longer. Something had to be done, and she could not count on her parents to help. She had to go to Mrs. Tuggle's house alone, confront her with what she knew, and tell her that unless she kept the crows away, she would tell her parents. If that didn't work, and Mrs. Tuggle knew she was bluffing, she would tell her that the town was already whispering about her and she had better watch her step.

It took almost a week to make the decision, and Lynn fully admitted to herself that she was afraid. It was frightening, first of all, to accuse a woman the family had known for some time, even though they did not know her well. Mrs. Tuggle always pretended to be friendly, and Lynn had always been polite. Now, to accuse her of something to her face. . . . What if it wasn't true? She could imagine how shocked and hurt and angry Mrs. Tuggle would be, and felt embarrassed. She knew the old woman would tell Mother, and the Morleys would ask Lynn how she could ever have thought of doing such an awful thing. But she was also terrified that perhaps Mrs. Tuggle would react angrily, perhaps even do something to her. And she wouldn't even have Marjorie there to protect her. She had to keep Mouse away no matter what.

She had already made up her mind that she would go some afternoon rather than at night. She would simply tell Mother that she was going for a walk and go straight up the hill. She would drink no tea, make no polite small talk, but come right to the point. It seemed so simple, but just thinking about it made her heart race.

On the third Saturday in October the time seemed right. Marjorie had gone downtown to help out at her father's store. Mother and Judith were baking bread. Steve was playing at a friend's house. And Mr. Morley was attending a meeting on the town master plan. Everybody was busy; no one would really miss her or feel the need to question her when she came back. The sun was out, and the fields, now brown and dry with autumn, shone gold. It was a very ordinary day, and Lynn did not feel quite so shaky.

As she started up the hill, however, she realized it might be easier to make her accusations when the old woman looked more creepy. If Mrs. Tuggle greeted her at the door with an apron on and the fragrance of cinnamon rolls in the air, how on earth could Lynn stick to her plan? She decided, therefore, to say the first words before she took one step inside—to set the mood before it was set for her. Then there would be no turning back.

How was it possible, she wondered, as she reached the top, for Mrs. Tuggle's house to look so ominous even in the middle of the afternoon? Instead of the spots of sunlight reflected on the old roof, she was more aware of the dark shadows made by the chimneys, and the deep caverns between the gables. While every-where else the town basked in the glory of a warm autumn day, Mrs. Tuggle's yard looked as though it had been passed by, as though the warmth could not penetrate the pines and thorn apple trees that surrounded the place. Perhaps she should have at least mentioned to Mother that she might stop in at Mrs. Tuggle's. What if no one ever saw her again?

She wanted to stop and go over her speech once more when she reached the iron fence, but she knew that if Mrs. Tuggle were watching, it would appear that she was hesitant and scared, which in fact she was. So she forced her feet to keep moving, her legs to keep walking. She opened the gate, closed it behind her, went up the narrow brick path to the porch, and reached for the knocker.

Here she couldn't help but pause, however. She had never liked the heavy door knocker, and on this particular day she like it even less. It was shaped to look like a troll with its tongue sticking out, and once Lynn had felt sure that the strange brass creature rolled its eyes. Quickly, before she could change her mind, she grabbed hold of it hard and banged it against the thick door. She liked the forceful sound of her banging, and was glad she had not tapped timidly.

She waited, listening for the telltale sound of footsteps inside. A minute passed. Nothing happened. She knocked again, even louder than before. Still no one came. She felt both disappointed and relieved. All this worry and suspense, and the woman wasn't even home.

Or perhaps she was. Maybe she had seen Lynn coming and refused to open the door.

Lynn walked over to a window and peered in. All was dark. But suddenly, in the reflection of the glass, she saw the eyes of Mrs. Tuggle grinning at her, and wheeling around, found herself face-to-face with the old woman.

chapter four

She wore no apron, and there was no fragrance of cinnamon buns about her. Wisps of gray hair that had worked themselves loose from the bun at the back hung down about her wrinkled cheeks, and her eyes seemed to glower in the deep recesses of their sockets. The grin had disappeared now, and she was unsmiling. Lynn suspected that the old woman already knew why she had come. The cat, huge and brownish, rubbed against a porch pillar and watched Lynn with yellow slits of eyes.

"I'd like to talk with you," Lynn said, and was sorry that her voice trembled slightly. She wanted to appear strong and confidant.

"Aye, and it's so fast you've been walking I couldn't catch up," Mrs. Tuggle said, observing her closely. "I saw you leave your house while I was still at the bottom of the hill, and the higher you walked, the faster you went." She moved over to the door and thrust her key in the lock. "Come in, my dear. I went to the butcher for some meat for Cat. I'll put it on a plate for him and fix our tea."

"I don't want any tea, Mrs. Tuggle," Lynn said determinedly, stepping inside. "I'd just like to talk to you for a few minutes, if you don't mind."

Mrs. Tuggle glanced at her out of the corner of her gray eye but continued on out to the kitchen. "Sit you down, Lynn girl. I'll be there directly."

Lynn went straight to the table in the corner. She wanted to look at the photograph of Mrs. Tuggle's brother one more time. She had even brought a magnifying glass in the pocket of her jeans so that she could study the spider mark on the boy's medallion and check it once more with the cat's. She reached the table and stopped. The photograph was gone.

Slowly she turned and sat down on an old velveteen chair, her heart thumping hard again, pulsating down through the palms of her hands. She could hear Mrs. Tuggle moving about the kitchen, talking to the cat, and pretty soon the teakettle began to whistle. Lynn began to feel angry. The old woman hadn't paid any attention to what she had said at all.

Finally there was the clatter of china cups on a tray, footsteps in the hallway, and Mrs. Tuggle entered the parlor. She put the tray on the small end table, poured two cups, and sat down.

"I don't want any tea," Lynn said again.

" 'Tis a special brew," Mrs. Tuggle said, without looking at her. "Branch water. I drew it myself from the creek. 'Tis clear and clean and boils up into a tasty pot."

"I don't *want* any!" Lynn said for the third time.

Mrs. Tuggle said nothing. She sat with her cup sheltered in her bony hands, the steam rising up in her face, her nostrils flaring as they sucked in the fragrant mist.

This is it, Lynn thought to herself. She had to say it now. Somehow her lips had to form those ugly words, and she had to speak aloud what she had been thinking all these months. This was the end of the pretending, the masquerade.

"Mrs. Tuggle," she said, her fingers trembling in her lap. "I came to tell you that I know exactly what you're up to and that you had better stop it."

The old lady did not look startled or shocked. She did not even blink, Lynn recalled later. The one green eye and the one gray eye fixed themselves on Lynn, and she went on drinking from her cup. The cat came out of the kitchen, stood in the doorway, and watched.

"What on earth are you talking about, child?" Mrs. Tuggle said at last, sounding grandmotherly again. "You make no sense at all."

Lynn began talking rapidly so she would not lose her resolve. "I think that I am making very good sense, Mrs. Tuggle. I know that you are into witchcraft, and that you have been working it on Marjorie Beasley. I think you should know that I won't let you hurt her."

The cat leaped up on the bureau, its tail lashing back and forth.

"Wherever did you get an idea like that?" Mrs. Tuggle exclaimed indignantly. "And why should I hurt little Marjorie? Does your mother know you're up here, Lynn, talking to me this way?"

"No, but if I need to tell her, I will," Lynn said defiantly. She was glad that the tremor had left her voice now. She felt excited inside, as though she were bursting almost, and the words came tumbling out. "I'll tell everything if I have to. I want you to stop those crows from following Marjorie around. Just leave us alone, especially her."

There was no smile on Mrs. Tuggle's face now. She put down the teacup and frowned. "You are talking nonsense, Lynn," she snapped. " 'Tis though the bogles had come and taken your mind, it is. What have the crows to do with an old lady like me?"

73

"Only you can answer that," Lynn said, and she was conscious of the cat's tail thumping angrily against the side of the bureau. "But Mouse and I saw you talking to the crows down by the creek. We know what you're trying to do. You tried to turn Judith into a witch last summer and it didn't work, and now you're after Marjorie. If you don't stop it, I'm going to tell Mr. Beasley and my parents and everyone in town, and they'll believe me, too, because they're already talking about you down at the courthouse." She stopped to catch her breath, realizing that she was talking far more confidently than she actually felt.

She had never seen the old woman's face look so terrible. If there had ever been softness in her eyes or pink on her cheeks or gentleness to her brow, there was none now.

"And what are the people saying about me, eh?" she asked sharply.

Lynn wondered if she should have brought that up, but it was too late now. "They're talking because there's no death certificate on file for your brother, and some are saying that maybe his death wasn't accidental at all. . . ." She stopped, not allowing herself to say more. Let Mrs. Tuggle worry about it. That would be even better.

"So you accuse me then, do you?" Mrs. Tuggle said coldly.

"I accuse you of being a witch," Lynn said, staring right back.

At that moment the cat gave such a shriek that Lynn jumped with fright. She wheeled around just as the animal leaped to the top of the mantel, then to the curtains, down to the sofa, and went streaking out of the room and up the stairs, screaming again its almost human cry.

"And see what you've done now, upset my cat!" Mrs. Tuggle scolded, frowning angrily. "*Ashamed* your mother would be of you, Lynn Morley!"

Lynn got up and walked out into the hall. "All I'm asking of you, Mrs. Tuggle, is that you leave us alone. It's hopeless, anyway, because Mouse knows all about you too, and she's got a book that tells about spells and things."

At that Mrs. Tuggle began to smile. The smile grew wider and wider, stretching her lips till the gums showed gray, and the gold tooth gleamed.

"I'm a lot older than you, Lynn girl, and much, much wiser," she said. "Take care that you don't turn the spirits against you." She laughed then, as if to herself, but after the door closed, Lynn could still hear the laughing, and it made the flesh on her arms rise up in small bumps.

She was halfway home before she even realized that her legs were moving. She slowed down and tried to catch her breath so she would not attract attention when she walked in.

It was done. She had said it, and felt both exhilarated and frightened. Things would never be the same between them again, she knew. If Mrs. Tuggle had ever had any fondness for Lynn, she had none now. But the old woman wouldn't tell her mother. Of that Lynn was sure. And she was positive now that her suspicions had been correct all along.

Mrs. Tuggle would have to leave them alone, too. She hadn't liked what Lynn had told her about the town gossip. She would have to be more careful of what she did, and could not afford to have two young girls telling their parents about her. For a brief moment Lynn felt a new wave of uncertainty rush through her, because she had already told her parents what she suspected, and they had not believed her. But Mrs. Tuggle need not know that. She and Mouse were safe from her, she felt sure. They could concentrate on other things. Like school. And skateboards. And whether or not they would go to camp together next summer.

"Lynn?" Mrs. Morley called. "I wondered where you went."

"Just out for a walk." Lynn tried to sound casual. "Bread done yet?"

"No. It has to rise again. We'll have some for dinner."

Lynn wished she could tell Mouse right away about

the visit to Mrs. Tuggle's, but knew she would not be home from the bookstore till evening. She went upstairs and lay on her bed, feeling suddenly exhausted from the confrontation. Maybe witchcraft works psychologically, she was thinking. If she were suggestible, she could suspect that Mrs. Tuggle had put a hex on her somehow—that her tiredness was actually the curse of death, and that she would grow weaker and weaker until she died. If she really believed it, she would be so paralyzed with fear that she would not eat; and if she stopped eating, she would get weaker yet, and finally she would really die. Well, she wouldn't let that happen to her.

At dinnertime, to assure herself that she was okay, she ate twice the usual amount—plenty of fried chicken, bread, even green beans.

"What'd you do this afternoon, jog a couple of miles?" Mr. Morley asked, as he watched the food on her plate disappear.

"Must be the fall weather," Mother said.

"If she keeps on eating that way, she'll be gross when she gets to junior high," Judith commented.

Lynn was halfway through dessert when the phone rang, and she answered it in the hall.

"Oh, Lynn," came Marjorie's voice. "The most awful thing happened. When I left the house this morning, I must have forgotten to close the back door tight. The wind blew it open and some animal got in. I left that book on the kitchen table because I was reading it at breakfast, and it's all clawed to pieces. It's in shreds!"

Lynn stood frozen to the floor. She could hardly speak. "The . . . book on . . . on spells and potions?"

"Yes. There's nothing left of it at all! And Daddy's furious. He says if I hadn't left it on the table, it couldn't have happened; and now I'm not even to touch any of his rare books, ever. He says if it hadn't been for you, I wouldn't even have been reading it in the first place. There are only a few copies of that book in the whole world, and he's so *mad*, Lynn!"

"No, no, no!" Lynn breathed. She felt sick. Things were getting worse, not better. "Oh, Mouse, I feel so awful."

"Well, I suppose he'll get over it in a couple of days, but he'll never feel better about that book. But Lynn, it's so scary. The animal didn't bother anything else. We know it was an animal because there were dark brown hairs on the table, like fur. Lynn, do you suppose it was? . . ."

"Yes, I'm sure of it," said Lynn.

It did not take long for Lynn to realize that her visit to Mrs. Tuggle's had not made things better, but had instead made them immeasurably worse.

First, the crows continued to follow Mouse. Mrs.

Tuggle had not been scared off at all by Lynn's threats.

Second, Lynn's babbling about the rare book on spells and potions had been a serious mistake. Now that the book was destroyed, Lynn and Mouse had lost the information they might need to protect themselves further; and to make it all worse, Mr. Beasley was angry at Lynn.

Third, it had put the old woman on guard. Now that she knew what Mouse and Lynn thought about her and what the townspeople were whispering, she would be craftier still.

And finally, Lynn felt that in accusing Mrs. Tuggle, she was committed to fighting the witchcraft alone. Her parents would certainly not have approved if they knew. If her father had thought at all that the old lady was dangerous, he would have done something himself. He would not have let Lynn go up to the house on the hill and make wild accusations. Instead he would have tried to discover the truth. But what else could she have done. She longed to confide in someone.

There was no school on Monday because of a state teacher's meeting. Mother went to her studio as usual, however, and left Judith and Lynn in charge of Stevie.

Lynn's little brother stood on the stairs flying a paper airplane over the banister to the floor below. When he tired of that, he sprawled out on the landing, staring up at the dust particles that streamed silently around in the light from the small window above.

"I wish I had a pet!" he bellowed loudly after a bit. "Bobby Lawson has a pet. Darrell Mills has a pet. Tony Corona has a pet. Gil Klaus has a pet. Alice Davis has a pet—"

"What kind would you want?" Lynn asked from downstairs in order to stop the recitation.

"Something I can play with. Something I could put in my bicycle basket and ride around."

Judith came down from upstairs, stepping over Stevie on the landing, and went into the kitchen for an orange.

"The problem with pets, Stevie," she called, sitting on the bottom step to peel it, "is that you have to take care of them. It would be fun for a while, but you'd get tired of all the work."

"I wouldn't get tired of it!" Stevie insisted. "Everybody in this family has somebody little-er than him except me."

Judith smiled. "You want to walk down to the pet store, just to see the puppies? We can't buy one, but I know Mr. Brickston would let you hold one."

Stevie jumped up. "Sure!"

"Want to come, Lynn? It's gorgeous out."

"I guess not," Lynn said. She had other things on her mind. And as soon as Judith and Stevie left, she set off up the hill to Mother's studio.

It was, Lynn had to admit, a cozy studio. An old

brick walk covered with moss led around to Mrs. Tuggle's backyard, where it branched off in two directions, one path leading to the old barn, and the other to the hen house. In a few minutes Lynn was standing outside the white building with the low roof, the windows clustered at each end. A little stove-pipe chimney stuck out the top, and a thin wisp of smoke trailed from it, indicating that the wood-burning stove inside was in operation. If only Mrs. Tuggle wasn't there talking. . . . Lynn gave a little knock on the rusty-orange painted door and went inside.

Mrs. Morley was sitting in a rocking chair beside the stove, her feet propped up on an opened drawer of her desk. The entire back wall, completely covered with built-in boxes where hens had once nested, now held writing supplies; large envelopes in one, small envelopes in another, manilla envelopes, carbon sets, bond paper, reference books, published books, old manuscripts, file folders—each of them had a special place. The frames around each window were orange like the door, and there was a small braided rug of orange, white, and yellow on the cement floor. And there, on the rug, lay Mrs. Tuggle's cat, its head upright, watching as Lynn came in.

"Well!" Mrs. Morley said, looking up. "It's not often I have a visitor way back here! Come on in, honey."

"Judith took Stevie down to the pet store, and I

thought maybe I could do some office work for you—filing, or something." Lynn sat on the corner of her mother's desk. The cat followed her with his eyes.

"What a nice thought! Let me think. . . . Ah! I've got just the job for you."

Mother got up, put her clipboard and pen on the rocker, and walked over to the low file cabinets beneath the windows at one end. She was wearing a pair of plaid slacks and a yellow sweater, and if Lynn hadn't known better, she would have thought that Mother had worked here in the chicken coop all her life. It was just right for her, warm and cozy, small and bright. The problem was that sometimes Mrs. Tuggle dropped in or invited Mother up to the house.

"Come here and I'll show you what needs to be done," Mrs. Morley said. She pulled open a drawer marked *Resource Material*. It was crammed full of file folders, and each one was labeled: Anthropology; Art; Creativity; Death; Dreams; ESP; Fears; Future; Gypsies; Hermits; Humor . . . Each folder was bursting with pages torn from magazines and newspapers.

"This is the file where I keep articles that might be useful to me in writing a certain story or book," Mother explained. "I'd like you to look over each article in each folder, trim the edges and cut off whatever part of the newspaper I don't need, then put the clipping back neatly in the folder. I'm running out of room because the folders are too thick. Here's the scissors and the wastebasket. You can stop whenever you get tired."

Lynn sat down on the braided rug cross-legged and spread the first folder out on the floor.

"Mother," she said, remembering why she had really come. "If I did something you didn't like . . . but I'd done it to save a friend, would you still be angry?"

Mrs. Morley put down her writing board again. "Now what kind of a question is that? You mean if you ruined a good set of clothes by jumping in the creek to rescue somebody? Of course I wouldn't be angry." She studied her daughter for a moment. "But I don't think that's what you had in mind."

"Well, not really," Lynn said. "I mean, if I said something that upset somebody . . ."

"We all say things we wish we hadn't," Mother said. "That doesn't concern me too much. Why? Who are you planning to upset?"

Lynn shook her head. "Nobody," she murmured.

Mrs. Morley laughed. "Lynn, I can read you like a book. You're suspecting poor Mrs. Tuggle again. You know, your suspicions are going to drive the old dear to doing something really witchy sometime, and then you'll be sorry! Sometimes people turn out to be what others accused them of being simply because it seems easier than forever defending themselves."

Lynn stared at the clippings there on the floor without really seeing them. Could it work the other way too, she wondered? Could a girl like Mouse be made to feel so weak and vulnerable that finally she believed she was helpless, and just gave in?

"The problem with having visitors here is that I don't get much work done," Mother said. "Let's see if we can have fifteen minutes of silence while I finish this one paragraph."

Lynn busied herself with the folders. She carefully cut the clippings out of the rest of the newspaper pages, stapled continued stories together, and put them back.

"Mother," she said, "does ? . . ." She stopped, realizing that she was interrupting again.

Mrs. Morley looked up expectantly. "Well, now that you've got my attention, what's the question?"

"I won't bother you any more," Lynn promised. "I just wanted to know if Mrs. Tuggle's cat comes here every day."

"Yes. He's usually waiting for me when I arrive in the morning or else comes by later and scratches at the door. I think Mrs. Tuggle lets him out at night so he can prowl around. He seems to enjoy stretching out here on the rug by the stove. But you know, that cat never really seems to relax or sleep. In fact, I've never seen him close his eyes. He's always watching. . . ."

For the next few days, Lynn stayed away from the Beasley house. If anything else happened—if the cat got in again—she did not want to be blamed for it.

Mr. Beasley laid the mischief on Lynn, Mouse, and squirrels, in that order.

In school on Friday, Lynn sat at the back of the room, toying with a paper clip. She had completed her math test and was waiting for the others to finish. She would have five minutes of uninterrupted thought, and she was glad. Her mind was always sharpest after a math test.

Her family, as she saw it, was divided three ways. Mother relied mostly on feelings—on sensing things, knowing them through intuition. Living, to her, was an art. When she did something, she did it rather spontaneously because it just seemed like a good thing to do, and Stevie and Judith were very much like her.

Father, however, was just the opposite. To him, life was a science. He planned things in advance. He did or said something because he had thought it out and knew the consequences. Inside his head, Lynn was sure, was a computer with plastic buttons and knobs and wheels, and everything he did was programmed down to whether he would eat a bite of steak next or a biscuit. Father could tell you exactly why he thought or believed anything at all. Everything he did was subjected to scientific inquiry, and if it didn't come out high on that score, he would have nothing more to do with it.

Lynn was somewhere in between. She believed

strongly in hunches and feelings and suppositions. But she also believed in stopping along the way to examine them—test them out to see if they made sense. If they didn't, it did not mean that they *wouldn't*. It just meant that she had to keep trying until evidence proved that her hunch had been right.

The topic to think about this morning was crows. Lynn had once thought that even if the crows followed Mouse about for the rest of her natural life, they wouldn't hurt her. After all, what could they do? Pick her up and carry her off? Hardly. Attack her? Possibly, but not likely. And what good would that do? Should either of these things happen, Mrs. Tuggle's witchcraft would have crossed over the line of coincidence and would be exposed for everyone to see.

Now Lynn believed that the crows had a more practical purpose than that. They were being used, she was sure, to frighten Marjorie, to convince her that she was the chosen one and that it was futile to escape. It was brainwashing, a wearing-down of the will, so that Mouse would decide that joining Mrs. Tuggle's coven was far better than always being terrified.

Lynn leaned forward, resting her chin on her hands. Maybe the old woman hadn't been as alone and inactive all these years as people had thought. Maybe she had made witches and warlocks out of some of the other girls and boys in town, and no one really knew about it. Maybe her emissaries of black magic were spreading all over the state of Indiana, and in going after Mouse, she was just doing what she'd been doing year after year. She hadn't been successful with Judith, but maybe that was just the way it was—win some and lose some—all in a month's work.

"Time," called the teacher. "Put your pencils down and pass your papers to the front of the room, please."

Lynn straightened up, handed her paper over the shoulder of the boy in front of her, and glanced across the room at Mouse. Marjorie was still on page two. She hadn't even started the third! That wasn't like her at all.

A crow cawed from somewhere outside, and Marjorie's pencil dropped out of her hand and onto the floor. She was staring out the window and didn't even notice.

I won't let Mrs. Tuggle take Mouse, Lynn told herself determinedly.

When Lynn reached home at three-thirty, Mother was in the music room going over some pieces on the piano.

"House cleaning," she said, trying to speak in time to the notes she was playing. "I found . . . all this old music . . . in the piano bench . . . and I'm deciding what to keep. . . ."

Lynn put her books down on the window seat and

88

went out to the kitchen for a handful of gingersnaps.

The music stopped. "I was always sorry I couldn't get you girls interested in music lessons," came Mother's voice from the next room. "I always wanted to be a great singer, and of course I'm not. But it *is* rather odd that neither you nor Judith wants to learn to play the piano."

Huh, thought Lynn. She'd always wanted to be a bareback rider in the circus, herself, but that was definitely out. She didn't have a horse. So she'd decided to be a psychiatrist instead and find out why she always wanted to be a bareback rider and why Mom always wanted to sing and why Mouse seemed so helpless about resisting Mrs. Tuggle.

"Did you see Stevie on the playground?" Mother asked when Lynn sauntered back through the hallway eating cookies.

"Didn't look."

"Well, he's probably playing there, I guess. He left about an hour ago, but didn't say where he was going." She stood up and piled some music on the stand by the piano. "Next time Marjorie comes over, have her take a look at these and see if she wants any of them."

Lynn took her books up to her room and lay down on her bed to study for a while. At four-thirty her mother came up, and Lynn could tell by her face that something was wrong.

"Lynn, I'm worried about Stevie. He's still not home. Would you run over to the school and see if he's playing there?"

Lynn slipped her feet back into her loafers, clattered down the two flights of stairs to the landing, then down to the first floor, and out the door. It *wasn't* like Stevie to go away like this. Usually he told them if he was even crossing the street. As he got older, though, he was getting more independent. Already, when he left kindergarten at noon, he often came straight home by himself instead of waiting for Mother on the corner. They had to expect things like this now and then.

Lynn rounded the corner and broke into a run, jogging the rest of the way. At the schoolyard two children were climbing the jungle gym.

"Have you seen Stevie?" she asked.

They shook their heads.

Going back, Lynn cut through the yards of the houses along the way until she arrived breathlessly at her own steps. A terrible feeling of dread was creeping up on her.

"He wasn't there, Mother," she said.

Mrs. Morley turned to Judith. "I'm going to search along the creek and see if he's playing down there. Lynn, try all the neighbors. And Judith, why don't you go to the pet shop. He just might have wandered down there since he enjoyed it so the other day. . . ."

Lynn went inside and phoned Mouse because she

was the only one of the two with a bike.

"Ask everyone you see, Mouse," she begged.

Then she started out herself, knocking on doors and stopping at houses where Stevie sometimes played. No one had seen him since he'd walked home with Mrs. Morley for lunch. Mother said he'd gone out to play in the side yard and then disappeared.

When half an hour had gone by with still no sign of Stevie, Lynn knew what she must do, and terror gripped her. Was it possible that her visit had so enraged the old woman that she had done something to Stevie? Look what the cat had done to Mr. Beasley's rare book! Maybe Mrs. Tuggle was far more powerful than Lynn had imagined. Maybe she had lured Stevie up to her house to hold him as hostage in exchange for the allegiance of Lynn and Mouse.

Lynn tried not to think about what she must do, but she knew she had to go straight up to Mrs. Tuggle's. She had to go to the door and say that she had come for Stevie. No, she would say that her mother had sent her for Stevie. In fact, her *father* had sent her, and she would say it direct in a no-nonsense kind of tone, as though they had known all along that Stevie was there, and they wanted him back immediately.

She reached the top of the hill, passed the clump of spruce trees, and then stopped. Marjorie's bike was leaning against Mrs. Tuggle's fence, and the gate was wide open.

chapter five

Even more alarming than the bicycle against the fence were the crows that circled the roof of the old house, indicating that Mouse was indeed inside. They looked like buzzards, Lynn thought—vultures making their last slow revolution before swooping down on the victim.

She ran up the walk, onto the porch, and grabbed the brass knocker, banging it hard against the door. Nothing happened. She banged again and again, panic rising inside her, and then began yelling: "Mouse! Mouse!"

The door opened, and Marjorie herself answered.

"What are you doing here?" Lynn demanded.

"Looking for Stevie."

There were more footsteps, and Mrs. Tuggle came through the dark hall. Her voice had the usual, lilting grandmotherly tone, but her eyes, as she faced Lynn, were sharp and hard, and there was no softness in the look which passed between them.

"Stevie has not been here at all," she said, "but if I see him, I'll be sure to send him running along home."

Lynn did not answer. "Come on, Mouse," she said, and, taking her arm, half pulled her down the sidewalk and out the gate.

Out of sight behind the thornapple tree, Lynn wheeled around and faced Marjorie.

"What were you *doing* in there all by yourself, Mouse? Why on earth did you come up here alone?"

Marjorie stared at her. "I was . . . was looking for Stevie, like you said."

"But you didn't have to go to Mrs. Tuggle's. And you certainly didn't have to go inside! *Why* did you go *inside*, Mouse?"

Marjorie's lips trembled. "I was asking for Stevie at the house across the street, and Mrs. Tuggle came out and called me over and took me inside and said she'd see if he was playing out back. . . ."

"She could have told you that on the porch, Mouse. Did she say anything else? *Think* now. Anything at all?"

Mouse looked pale and scared. "She . . . she said

she liked my ring . . . and asked to try it on. . . ."

Lynn grabbed Mouse by the shoulders and shook her back and forth till the glasses slipped off her nose and hung by one ear.

"Mouse! Are you crazy? Are you absolutely nuts? Don't you know what she's up to?"

Marjorie started to cry, and Lynn was instantly sorry. Huge blobs of tears rolled down out of Marjorie's eyes, matting her lashes, and dropped off her chin onto her green jacket.

Lynn put one arm around her and they sat down by the fence.

"Oh, Mouse, I'm sorry. I didn't mean it. I'm just so scared and worried about you, and . . . you *didn't* take the ring off, did you?"

"No. You knocked at the door just then." She started to cry again. "But I might have. Oh, Lynn, she can talk me into anything. Anybody can talk me into anything! I'm nothing but marshmallow inside!"

Lynn put both arms around her and rocked her gently.

"Mouse. Please listen to me. You're stronger than you think. You've got to believe in yourself. You can stay away from Mrs. Tuggle if you really try. You mustn't ever see her alone. Never come here again by yourself. The fact that she wanted you to take off the ring proves that it *is* some kind of protection against her, and she knows it. That's why she sent her cat to destroy the book. Even if it's only psychological protection, even if you're only stronger because you *think* the ring makes you stronger, it's harder for her to get you into her corner. Don't you see?"

Mouse continued to sob. She put her face down on her knees and rocked back and forth.

"Lynn, I'll never make it! I'm tired of fighting it. What's the use? Sometimes she just seems like a harmless old lady. She was so sweet and kind to me in there, and she seemed so concerned, and said if I ever wanted to talk to somebody like a m . . . mother, I could just come up here anytime. . . ."

Lynn felt as though all the blood had drained out of her body and left ice in its place. Of course, Mrs. Tuggle was going to play mother to Mouse; and Marjorie, wanting it so desperately, could hardly refuse. What could Lynn possibly do about it? *She* couldn't be her mother. Should she write Mrs. Beasley and tell her to come back, that Mouse needed her? No, she knew that wouldn't work. Then Mr. Beasley would *never* let Lynn in the house again.

She sat with her arms around Mouse until the sobbing finally stopped. Mouse seemed so tiny, so vulnerable—like Stevie, almost. And suddenly she remembered her lost brother and leaped up.

"Oh, Mouse! I forgot all about Stevie! If anything's happened to him. . . ."

"He wasn't in her house, Lynn. We looked."

95

The girls jumped on Marjorie's bike. Lynn sat on the seat, her hands on Marjorie's waist, and Mouse stood upon the pedals. They went careening out into the street and down the hill to the Morleys'.

Lynn felt that things were closing in on her. How could she possibly protect Mouse and Stevie at the same time? How could she fight off crows and cats or do anything at all if no one believed her?

When they were a block from the house, they could see Judith standing out on the porch waving to them and calling.

"We found Stevie," she said as they rode up onto the sidewalk. "He'd followed Mrs. Tuggle's cat out in the meadow and was playing down by the creek."

Lynn felt both relieved and frightened as she walked in the house beside Mouse. Stevie was safe for the moment, but he had known better than to go to the creek. He'd been told as long as he could remember that he should never go there alone. The cat had lured him there. The cat was evil, and Lynn felt a deep hatred for the animal stir up somewhere inside her. The cat, even more than the crows, was her enemy. Mrs. Tuggle would get at her any way she could, through Stevie, even.

If Mrs. Morley knew that Mouse needed extra mothering that day, it was by intuition only. Whatever, as soon as the girls walked in, she grabbed them both and hugged them hard. It was, Lynn realized, mostly a reaction to having found Stevie safe and sound, even though he'd been sent to his room for the rest of the day.

"Marjorie, I haven't seen you for at least a week," Mother said. "How are you, dear?" She looked at her more closely, and Lynn wondered if she noticed the streaks that the tears had left on her face.

"Okay," Mouse said. How easy it was to lie, Lynn was thinking. Why did people always say *okay* or *fine* when they weren't at all? Why did they have to pretend things were going great when they were going terribly? But if Mouse had answered, "I'm lonely, Mrs. Morley, and the witches are after me," would it have done any good? Would anyone have believed her?

"I found some old piano music the other day when I was housecleaning, and I thought of you right away," Mother said, putting an arm around Mouse and leading her into the music room. "If you like any of it, you can take it home with you."

They sat down together on the piano bench, and Mrs. Morley opened one of the scores. "You play the treble clef and I'll play the bass and it will give you an idea of how it sounds."

"I'm not very good," Mouse grinned, but she liked the idea of a duet.

"Neither am I," said Mother. "We'll make a great pair."

If only they could keep Mouse here with them, Lynn

thought as she sat on the window seat and watched Marjorie and her mother laughing together. If they could sort of adopt her, to keep until Mrs. Tuggle died or something. But she knew that would never work. Mr. Beasley was far too fond of his daughter to give her up. No, the most important thing was to see that Mouse kept that ring on her finger, no matter what. And because they knew knew that Mrs. Tuggle wanted it, things seemed scarier than ever.

That evening, Lynn did something she had not intended to do. She told her parents what had been happening. Some of it, that is. She knew how her mother regarded the idea of witchcraft. And she knew how disgusted her father was at people who gossiped about Mrs. Tuggle, or anybody else for that matter. Accusations were not permitted in a courtroom without evidence, he always said, and he often mistook the Morley house for a courtroom. But once in a while, Lynn thought, she caught a glimpse of uncertainty in her parents' eyes, a trace of doubt in their voices when they spoke of the old woman. And so, when Lynn walked in the kitchen that evening and found them standing at the window, their arms around each other, they seemed so relaxed and good-humored that she realized if ever she was going to tell them, now was the time. Things were happening too fast, and perhaps even Stevie was in danger. She just had to tell someone.

"Good apple," Mr. Morley said, holding a winesap up for inspection. "Ought to try one, Lynn. I picked these up at Grossman's market. First of the season." He sat down in a chair by the table and stretched out his legs while Mother looked over some shopping coupons on the counter.

"I don't want anything more to eat," Lynn said. She sat down across from him and tucked her feet under her. "Dad, I'm scared."

Mother turned around. "Of what?"

"If I tell you, could we have a serious discussion without anybody getting mad?"

"I'll try my best," her father promised.

Lynn took a deep breath. "Okay. I know how you both feel about Mrs. Tuggle. I know you like her, Mother, and think she's a sweet old lady. And I agree with you, Dad, that people shouldn't go around spreading gossip unless they have proof. But that doesn't stop the scared feeling."

Mr. Morley took another bite of apple and surveyed his daughter quizzically. "So you're afraid of Mrs. Tuggle—a frail old lady like her?"

"Yes."

"Why? What can she possibly do to hurt you, Lynn?"

"I think she's trying to get Mouse into her coven. . . ." She stopped as both parents began to smile. "I know it sounds funny, but awful things are happening. Marjorie and I were down by the creek one day, and Mrs. Tuggle was walking along the other side and she called to the crows and nine of them flew down and landed on her arms."

"Really?" Mother said, interested. "I didn't know crows could be that tame."

"Neither did I. But she talked to them, Mother, like they all had names."

"Well, I don't know, Lynn," her father said. "Old women who live in cities often go to the park to feed and talk to the pigeons. You want us to burn her at the stake for that?"

"Dad, ever since then those nine crows have been following Mouse around, and she's doing worse and worse in school. Every day they follow her from tree to tree, and she's scared to death. We went down to her father's store one day to tell him about it and the crows followed us down there, but when he came outside to look, they were gone. It's witchcraft!"

"Now, Lynn." Mr. Morley threw his apple core in the sink and leaned forward. "You're an intelligent girl. Think about what you just said. It sounds pretty kooky, doesn't it? You want us to believe that nine crows are following Marjorie Beasley around, yet no one can see them but you?"

"And Marjorie! And once somebody at school noticed them. I mean, they're not invisible or anything.

It's just that as soon as someone else notices them, they fly away."

Mother stood leaning against the refrigerator, her eyes on Lynn, her face anxious. Then she gave her husband a hurried glance and sat down at the table between them.

"Sweetheart," she said, and her voice was soft and gentle, the way she had sounded when Lynn had been ill with strep throat. "We love you, and we're concerned about you. I think it's quite possible that there are strange things about Mrs. Tuggle that you, being very observant, have noticed, and that Marjorie, being very suggestible, has seemed to notice too. Mrs. Tuggle is rather eccentric, and unless one sees her every day as I do, it's easy to suppose she's a witch, I guess. Imagination can play strange tricks. But I really think we've reached a point where your ideas are not really normal—"

"Mother, believe me! It's not just an idea. It's fact! It's really true! The crows are there!"

Mrs. Morley stared down at her hands on the table and fell silent.

"Lynn." Mr. Morley took it up now. "Is there anything else you're worried about these days besides Mrs. Tuggle? Anything at all that you haven't told us about apart from witches and stuff? Are there problems at school, maybe?"

"No! What else would I be worried about?"

Again the look passed between her parents, and Lynn sat wondering.

"You know, Lynn, there's a school psychologist for the county who is great at helping boys and girls work out problems that are troubling them," Mother said. "Sometimes people have worries they're not even aware of, and when they're gradually helped to talk about them with someone outside the family—someone qualified to help—things don't seem so frightening anymore. I think it might be a good idea to arrange a conference. Dad and I could go along if you like, or you could go alone, but I. . . ."

Lynn started to cry, more out of frustration than anything else. "I don't have any worries except Mrs. Tuggle and Mouse and what's going to happen to her," she sobbed angrily. "You just can't understand what I'm talking about! You can't believe that I'm telling the truth."

She jumped up and started for the hallway. "Someday, if anything happens to Mouse, everyone is going to remember that I tried to warn you!" And then, with tears streaming down her cheeks, she bolted up the stairs and sank down on the landing, burying her face in her arms. She hadn't even told them the rest. She hadn't told about the photograph of Mrs. Tuggle's brother and the cat's spider-mark medallion. She hadn't told them how she had gone to Mrs. Tuggle's and accused her of being a witch, and how the old woman hadn't denied it. She hadn't told them how the cat clawed up Mr. Beasley's book on spells and potions or how Mrs. Tuggle tried to get the ring off Marjorie's finger. She hadn't even mentioned her fears for Stevie. She was ashamed of herself. She had asked that they have a serious discussion without anyone getting mad, and it was she who had left the room. If she was really mature and reasonable, she would march right back down there and tell them the rest. . . .

But then she heard her parents' voices from the kitchen, and sat listening.

". . . but why are you angry at *me?*" Mother's voice was plaintive.

"Oh, I'm not angry at anybody," Mr. Morley responded gruffly. "I'm just disgusted that we haven't done a better job of keeping her imagination in check. She ought to get out more, make new friends. Put two girls together like Lynn and that bird-brained Beasley kid, throw in an idea, and you've got an explosion."

"I think Marjorie's a very nice girl," Mother defended.

"I didn't say she wasn't. But she'll believe anything. Lynn could make her believe the sky is celery soup if she tried. When Lynn gets an idea in her head, there's no stopping her."

"Well, if you're not angry at me, you certainly sound like it by the tone of your voice." There was the noise of a chair scraping the floor and Lynn knew that her mother was standing up. "Is it my fault that Lynn doesn't spend her time going to parties and playing soccer or something?"

"No, but I think it's interesting that she didn't get these ridiculous ideas about Mrs. Tuggle till you started writing that book about witches."

"That's not true!" Mother's voice was angry now. "I got the idea from her! If it hadn't been for her imagination, that book would never have got off the ground."

"So you just reinforce it," Father said. "As soon as she started talking about the idea, we should have sat on it. Instead, the whole house is inhabited by imaginary spirits, and—"

"What do you want me to do, Richard? Give up writing? Be afraid to explore an idea for fear Lynn will pick it up and blow it all out of proportion? Is that? . . ."

Lynn scrambled up from the floor of the landing and rushed upstairs to second, then up the narrow stairway to her room at the top, flinging herself on the bed. Why had she ever brought the subject up? What made her think she could ever tell them? If she didn't be careful, they might separate just like Mr. and Mrs. Beasley had done, and it would be all her fault! She would never mention it again. Never, never. She would pretend that all her fears were over and that she and Mrs. Tuggle were friends. Whatever happened from now on, she was on her own. She was even more alone than she had suspected.

"What's the matter?"

Lynn wondered if she'd been asleep, because she hadn't heard Judith come upstairs. She rolled over. Judith was standing there with a book she'd been reading on her side of the curtain.

"You've been lying there for twenty minutes," Judith said. "Sick or something?"

"No, I'm okay." Lynn sat up. "Have you ever tried to explain something to Mom and Dad and they just couldn't understand what you meant?"

Judith thought for a minute. "Yes."

"What?"

"I tried to tell them last week that I'm in love with Doug Heinzelman, and I could tell they didn't believe me."

"How could you tell?"

"By what they said!" Judith leaned against Lynn's dresser and flopped her long black hair over her shoulder. "Mother said that I have a lot of living yet to do and not to be too upset if something happened between Doug and me. I mean, wasn't that a dumb thing to say right after I told her we were in love?

Already she's talking about our breaking up."

Yes, Lynn thought, that was a dumb thing to say; but just because a person was an adult didn't mean they couldn't do anything stupid. Besides, breaking up could happen to anybody. If the Beasleys did it, it could happen to Judith and Doug Heinzelman too, or even Mom and Dad. Oh, why had she said a word about Mrs. Tuggle and made them mad at each other?

"So what were you trying to explain to them that they didn't understand?" Judith wanted to know.

"Oh, nothing." Lynn got up and tried to change the subject. "They just don't understand Mouse very well, that's all."

"Who does?" Judith laughed. "*Nobody* understands that girl, not even her father!" Then she felt she'd said too much and apologized. "Oh, I didn't mean it like that. I feel sorry for her, really. If she'd just *think* before she put her clothes on in the morning, she wouldn't look so much like a refugee, that's all."

As Judith started for the stairs, something darted into the room and streaked behind the curtain.

"What was that?" Lynn asked.

"It looked like that big cat of Mrs. Tuggle's. Honestly, that animal has been coming in here like he owns the place!" She shrugged and started downstairs. "Never did care about cats one way or the other."

Lynn stood still and waited till she heard Judith

reach the floor below. Then she cautiously walked across to the heavy curtain, pulled it aside, and entered Judith's bedroom. The cat was nowhere in sight. Slowly she circled the room, watching . . . waiting for the slightest sound. She would not tolerate the cat coming here.

She knelt down and looked under the bed. Two gleaming eyes looked back.

"Get out! Shoo!" Lynn said, and wiggled the bed. The cat didn't move.

Lynn went down to the second floor bedrooms and got a mop from the closet. When she came back up, she thrust the mop under the bed, poking at the cat.

"Get out!" she commanded. The cat backed away and settled down again on its haunches.

The helplessness that Lynn had felt earlier was turning now into anger. How dare this animal disobey her? How dare it come into their house? In fury, she shoved the bed to one side and began swinging wildly with the mop, this way and that.

The cat gave a shriek and flew out from under the bed. It crouched against the wall, its back arched, hissing.

Lynn went over to the door and closed it. Then she opened Judith's window, unlatched the storm window and swung it open and approached the cat again.

"Get out, you evil thing," she said through clenched

teeth as the cat watched her move. "Don't you ever come here again." The cat didn't budge.

Suddenly, in fury, Lynn lunged at it with the mop and whacked it hard on one side. The cat spun toward the window, a strange, almost-human cry in its throat. It scrambled up on the window ledge and turned to face Lynn, its hair on end, eyes huge and yellow.

Lynn walked toward it, holding the mop in front of her.

"I know who you are," she said, "and I know what you're trying to do." The cat leaned forward, body balancing on the windowsill as though it were going to jump down into the room again. Then it opened its mouth and snarled.

Lynn swung. The mop hit the cat full force, knocking it straight through the open window and onto the roof of the porch below. It paused only a moment on its toes, as though suspended in flight, and then, propelled by the momentum of its fall, leaped onto the grass below, where it stood, eyes upward, tail lashing wildly.

"That'll teach you!" Lynn said, and pulled the storm window shut. As she did so, the cat uttered another noise that Lynn could not describe even to Mouse. It was a half-wail, half-laugh, that sounded as if it were coming from the throat of a boy.

She slumped down on the floor, her heart racing.

Maybe she did need the school psychologist after all. When people go bananas, she thought, they don't even know it. They think they're talking sense when everyone around them knows they're talking nonsense. They see things and hear things that no one else can see or hear.

No, she said aloud. *Even if nobody else in the world believes me, I've got to believe in myself.* She had heard a human voice from the throat of the cat, and it was the most terrifying sound she had ever heard.

chapter six

Autumn died, and the nothingness of November took its place. The trees, which had been bushy with clumps of red and gold a few weeks earlier, stood bedraggled with a dry, colorless leaf here and there. Heaps of dead leaves, rotting from the rains, covered sidewalks and lawns, and the fields which had blazed gold under the October sun were now brown and nondescript. Everything seemed to have turned gray—the streets, the trees, the houses in the dark November light, and most of all the sky.

Lynn made a determined effort to be natural and cheery when she was around her parents, to cause them no concern, avoiding all hints that she was worried.

She went to school each day, ate a snack when she got home, did her math, and went out walking with Mouse, arriving home in time for dinner, full of talk about her teachers and studies and how she was doing in gym class.

Her parents were relieved. So thorough was her act that one evening her father forgot his own precautions and said to his wife, "They turned the matter of the missing death certificate over to the sheriff for a routine check." Lynn didn't respond at all.

"I'll have another piece of pumpkin bread," was all she said, seeming to have ignored the conversation altogether.

As Father passed the bread, he couldn't help but say, "You seem more yourself these days, Lynn. As if you're not as worried as you used to be."

"About Mrs. Tuggle?" Lynn said casually. "I'm too busy at school to even think about her."

"That's my girl," Father said jovially and exchanged a relieved smile with Mother.

Great, thought Lynn. At least her parents wouldn't have to quarrel about her any more. At least *one* good thing was happening.

At the same time, Lynn wondered if Mother was completely convinced of the change in her. She noticed that Mrs. Morley was watching her more closely than usual, studying her reaction, for example, if a tree branch scratched the window or a crow cawed outside. Lynn knew she was being observed and pretended to be startled at nothing.

Inside herself, however, Lynn was shriveling with fear. The nine crows continued to hover, and the bare November trees made their presence even more noticeable. One afternoon, as Mouse walked home with her, Lynn felt that the crows were so obvious, following along overhead, that anyone who happened to look up would not fail to notice them. If only Mother were watching at that moment, she would see them, too. Maybe, just maybe, if they were still there when they reached the porch, she would tell Mouse to wait outside and go in herself and have Mother look out. Just as they reached the steps, however, Mother came out on the porch with Stevie, and the crows silently winged their way on over the house out of view, as though controlled by a lead crow who was half-human.

Even worse, Stevie had taken a liking to Mrs. Tuggle's cat, despite being punished for having followed it down to the creek. Sometimes when Lynn came home from school, she found him sitting on the front steps, stroking the big animal.

"Look what I found, Lynn," he said one day, his round face beaming with the discovery. "It's a necklace on the cat!" He examined it carefully. "It looks like a spider, so that's what I'm gonna call this old cat. Spider.

Isn't that a good name?"

Lynn stood on the sidewalk facing the cat. It stared back, tail swishing. "That's an excellent name, Stevie," she said. "It fits perfectly."

"Yeah, 'cause *some* spiders are brown, aren't they?"

"Yes, and some are cunning and crafty and poisonous."

"You don't like spiders, do you, Lynn?"

"Some of them I don't." She walked on up the steps, and as she passed, the fur on the cat's back rose stiffly, ruffling thickly about the neck, and then lay flat again when the front door closed behind her. Lynn watched it through the window in the music room. Was it possible that the animal was half-human, that inside the skin and fur there was a remnant of a human brain that had been programmed against her?

Cat and Mouse. The phrase stuck in her mind, and she couldn't rid herself of it. Her hands grew cold. Marjorie was no match for an animal like this one. Not now, especially. Things were going worse for Mouse every day. The gym teacher had scolded her just that morning because she hadn't pressed her gym suit.

It's a wonder she's even wearing a gym suit at all, Lynn had thought to herself, wincing as the teacher's harsh voice rang out over the gym. *If the teacher knew how many times I've reminded Mouse to get that suit washed and back to school on time, she'd go easier on her.*

She wondered if she should talk to the teacher later about it and tell her the problems Mouse was having at home. But she knew she couldn't go on forever offering excuses. Eventually Marjorie had to face the fact that her mother probably wasn't coming back, no matter how much she loved Mouse. In the meantime, Lynn had to fill in and be the best friend she could.

What Mouse needed help with most at the moment was a science project. Everyone in class had to collect twenty specimens of common weeds and identify and label them. Lynn had managed to collect a dozen just by keeping her eyes open on the way to school. But Marjorie's eyes were on the trees, not the ground, and she hadn't even started the project. So on this particular afternoon, Lynn suggested they go out in the meadow after school and collect the specimens together.

About four o'clock they headed across the meadow with a paper bag between them, following the creek as it wound around between the old cemetery on one side and the hill on the other.

"You know what, Lynn?" Mouse confided as they tramped through the crisp brown grass that crackled underfoot. "Last night I dreamed that I ran away, and when I woke up this morning, it didn't seem like such a bad idea."

"That's dumb, Mouse, where would you go?"

"Cincinnati, maybe. To live with Mother."

"If your mother thought that was the best place for

you, she would have taken you there."

"But maybe if she knew what was happening to me here, she'd let me stay with her."

"She might." Lynn fell silent. "But your father would be frantic," she said finally. "He'd have everyone in the whole Midwest looking for you."

"I could hide out," Mouse offered. "Freight trains and stuff."

Lynn tried to imagine it. *Lost: one short girl, straight brown hair, large glasses, skinny legs, dressed in yellow jeans and a huge purple poncho.* Anyone who saw Mouse would never forget her.

"What if the crows came with you?"

"Oh, Lynn, don't say that."

"Well, don't talk about running away, then. I'd miss you like anything. And your Dad would go nuts. You just might move a whole pack of trouble to Ohio along with you. We'll stick it out together. As long as you keep that ring on your finger and stay away from Mrs. Tuggle I don't see how she can really do anything. After a while she'll figure she's just not getting anywhere and give up, like she did with Judith. Especially now that the sheriff's investigating the death of her brother. Not that he'll find out anything, of course, but it just might make her more cautious. After all, she's not about to come knocking on your door and just snatch you away."

Lynn knelt down and removed a cocklebur from her sock, dropping it in the sack. They had already picked up some thistle, some dock, and a few pieces of Indian mallow. Mouse saw some milkweed growing halfway down the bank by the creek, stepped over the edge, and reached down.

There was a sudden sound of footsteps behind them. Lynn looked around. Mrs. Tuggle was walking straight toward them in big, steady strides, her face intent, eyes glimmering, her thin lips quivering slightly, holding a heavy stick in one hand. Where she came from, Lynn did not know, unless she had been hiding somewhere in the bushes.

"M . . . Mouse!" Lynn cried out as the old lady came at them. Marjorie lifted her head just as Mrs. Tuggle reached the bank. She gave a little cry, lost her balance, and tumbled backwards into the swirling water below.

It happened so quickly that Lynn did not see Mouse tumble into the creek until she heard the splash.

"Mouse!" she screamed, dropping the sack and scrambling down the bank sideways.

Below in the water, Marjorie struggled to get her head up, arms flailing, legs kicking. It was here that the current seemed to move in circles, that a mist rose up from the surface of the creek, and here that the water was deepest of all. Lynn did not know whether Mrs. Tuggle was coming down the bank behind her or not. She could only think of reaching Marjorie, but by the time she got to the water's edge. Mouse was upright once more, clinging to the roots of a tree that projected out from one side.

At that moment Mrs. Tuggle's voice sounded in the air above them. Lynn looked up. The old woman stood holding the stick out over the water. The lead crow from the nine in the trees overhead had flown down and was perched on one shoulder. Mrs. Tuggle's eyes, small and terrible, were fixed on Mouse, and she was mumbling something that Lynn could not understand —words of another language, Hebrew, perhaps, or Greek. And then suddenly she reached down and held the stick out toward Mouse.

"Here, my girl, catch on and pull yourself up before you catch your death," she clucked. "My goodness, two girls out and about without watching where they're stepping. . . ."

Spluttering, and still dazed by the tumble, Mouse grabbed hold of the stick, and Mrs. Tuggle hoisted her up the bank. Lynn was amazed at the old woman's strength. She leaped up and pulled Mouse away.

"Come on, Mouse. Let's get you home so you can change."

"I've a fire going in my parlor," Mrs. Tuggle crooned,

ignoring Lynn. "Come up to the house and dry your-self, my dear. And a spot of tea will be good for you."

"No, thank you," Lynn said coldly, tugging at Mar-jorie's arm.

Mrs. Tuggle slowly turned and faced Lynn. "Has the girl no tongue to answer for herself?"

No, the cat's got it, thought Lynn, but she said noth-ing. She had one arm around Marjorie's shoulders and was leading her away. She could feel Mouse trembling and walked on faster. The crows overhead flew lower than usual, cawing raucously, their shadows spotting the ground.

When they had left Mrs. Tuggle far behind, Mouse's head flopped over on Lynn's shoulder.

"I feel so tired," she said. "Like I can hardly walk. All of a sudden I feel weak and sleepy, as though I just don't care about anything."

"You've probably got a chill," Lynn said, not believing it herself. They walked on, but Marjorie's feet dragged, and she leaned heavily against Lynn. Something seemed to have happened to her back there. Was it the incanta-tion Mrs. Tuggle had intoned over her when she fell in? Was it a power of some sort, transmitted through the stick that Mrs. Tuggle had been carrying? Or was it all psychological?

"That was no accident, Mouse," Lynn said at last. "She wanted you in that water. Maybe she wanted both of us to fall in, I don't know. I can't say that she pushed us, but it was the next thing to it."

"Yes," Mouse said weakly. "It's the water. I'm sure of it. There was something in the book about bodily transformation. Something about a person being dipped in water or milk before he could be turned into anything else. Well, I was sure dipped, but I'm still me. I think."

Lynn frowned. "Did you remember that it's creek water Mrs. Tuggle uses for her tea? She told us so. And remember how sleepy you got the first time you drank it?"

"Oh, Lynn, if she's got the whole creek in her power, how can we fight it? She could get half the town under her spell just by scaring people into falling in."

Lynn tried to laugh it off.

"I'm sure it would take more than that, Mouse. Remember what you said about having to want the power of witchcraft more than anything else at one particular moment? Most folks, when they fall in a creek, want more than anything else to get out, that's all."

But inside, Lynn felt sick with fear. Maybe the effects of the water wouldn't show up right away. Maybe first it was tea, then a dip in the creek, and slowly, bit by bit, Marjorie's will to resist would be washed away until she was willing to do anything Mrs. Tuggle required of her. Suddenly she remembered the ring.

"Mouse," she cried, "have you still got the ring?"

Mouse made no move to lift her hand and see. She seemed hardly to have heard. Lynn grabbed her hand and looked. The ring was still there. She felt weak with relief.

When they reached the Beasley house, Lynn helped Mouse get off her wet clothes and crawl into bed.

"I'll go back and get that sack," she said. "We only needed about four more specimens, and I'll pick those up on the way home. Come by the house tomorrow about twenty minutes early, and I'll help you label yours. Okay, Mouse? Are you awake?"

"I'm awake," came a voice from under the covers; but it didn't sound very awake.

Lynn went outside, making sure that the front door was locked behind her. Then she cut back to the meadow again, picking up Jimson weed, toadflax, and goldenrod as she went, retracing her steps along the creek till she caught sight of the paper bag down near the water.

She had just climbed down to get it and was turning around when a shadow fell over her. Thinking that Mrs. Tuggle had come back again, this time for her, she jerked her head up, but saw—instead of the old woman —the nine crows, like a dark cloud, circling overhead. She hugged the paper sack to her and climbed back up the bank, walking rapidly once she reached the top. When she came to the footbridge that crossed the lowest part of the creek, she almost ran across it and up through the field in the direction of the Morley garden.

There was something different about the crows now. They made no noise at all—no cawing, no loud flapping of wings. Only the dark shadow that fell on the ground before her reminded her that they were there.

And suddenly they swooped. Like fighter planes plunging from the sky, they came at her. The lead crow sailed by, his wing tips grazing her cheek. On all sides she could feel birds passing, feel the sting of their slashing wings on her arms, hear the whistle of the wind as they flew past her ears. As she turned to see if they had gone, she saw them forming again, and again they attacked, their bodies closer still, like angry missiles, hurling themselves at her back.

Screaming with fright, Lynn fell face forward on the ground and covered her ears with both hands. She was sure she would be killed. They would rip her flesh to shreds, just as the cat had ripped the book on spells and potions.

But they did not come again. Instead they rose in the air, cawing raucously in unison, like demons shrieking compliance to an unseen master. And as Lynn slowly turned to watch, they fell into place behind the lead crow and made their way to Marjorie's again to wait.

For a few moments Lynn did not get up. She was trembling so hard she was not sure her legs would move. It was not just Mrs. Tuggle whom the girls were fighting, but the crows and cat as well. Mouse talked as though she had already given up, as though it were useless even to try. For a brief moment Lynn felt it too—felt how easy it would be just to go to Mrs. Tuggle's and drink her tea and do whatever she asked of them. No more crows following them about from tree to tree, no more cat prowling about in the house. No fuss, no worry—simple, mindless robots who did as they were told.

As the shivering stopped, however, she realized that this kind of thinking played right into Mrs. Tuggle's scheme. It wasn't Mrs. Tuggle's stick or her incantations that were so powerful, but the fear they produced. Once the old woman had paralyzed her victims with terror and trembling, she could make them do whatever she wished.

Lynn pulled herself up quickly and walked the rest of the way up the hill to the house. She wasn't about to give up yet. The harder the old woman fought, the harder she would resist.

"What *happened?*" Mother said, turning around as Lynn passed her in the hall.

Lynn stopped and looked at herself in the mirror. There were strange marks on both cheeks where the crows' wing tips had grazed her. Pieces of grass and weeds were sticking to her hair and on her jacket.

How Lynn wanted to tell her! How she longed to throw herself in her mother's arms and tell her she was frightened, to beg for protection. But how would she ever be believed? How could she honestly say that Mrs. Tuggle was responsible for Marjorie's fall in the creek? How could an eleven-year-old girl just walk in her own house and insist she had been attacked by nine demon crows, scratches or not? And she remembered the night her parents had quarreled about her. . . .

"We had to collect twenty weed samples for a science project," she said, but she could not control the slight quiver in her voice. "Some of the places you wouldn't believe! Mouse and I got all scratched up."

"Good heavens, it looks as if something got hold of you," Mother said. "I just wish your teacher would think before she gives out these assignments."

"Well, she didn't exactly tell us to go climbing along by the creek. It just seemed a good place to get all the weeds at once."

Lynn thought she had done a pretty good job of being casual, but when she was examining her cheeks in the bathroom mirror, Mother came to the doorway and studied her again. Twice she opened her mouth as if to say something, then thought better of it.

"What do you want?" Lynn said finally, wondering.

Mrs. Morley sighed. "Lynn, I know this sounds dumb, and I certainly don't want to get those old worries of yours started again, but I need to know: do those marks on your cheeks have anything to do with Mrs. Tuggle?"

Lynn's heart beat faster. "What do you mean?" she asked, stalling for time.

"Just what I said. Oh, I know my imagination works overtime the same as yours. But I want to know. They *don't*, do they?"

"Don't what?"

Mrs. Morley was exasperated. "Have anything to do with Mrs. Tuggle. The scratches! She didn't attack you, did she?"

"Why would she do a thing like that?" Lynn asked innocently.

Mother laughed, relieved. "For no reason at all, dear. I'm sorry I said a thing." She turned to go, then paused again. "You know, the best thing to do, I think, is just stay away from her. I mean, no one else in the family seems as affected by her as you do, so I think I'd feel better if you just stayed away from up there. Okay?"

"Sure."

Lynn waited till she heard her mother going downstairs. Then she leaned forward and stared at her face in the mirror. Could Mother be having second thoughts about the old woman? Could she have noticed things lately, seen things, that disturbed her, too? Was the attack by the crows the extent of the old woman's power, or were there more things yet to come?

There was more to come. On Saturday, Lynn had risen early and was frying an egg for herself when the phone rang. Everyone else was sleeping. She turned off the stove and ran into the hall. Marjorie's voice came over the line, weak and faraway. Lynn's first thought was that Mrs. Tuggle had abducted her and thrown her down a well.

"Mouse! Where are you?"

"Listen, Lynn, I can't talk very loud because I don't want Daddy to hear."

"What? I can hardly hear you. What's the matter?"

"I've got to talk to you."

"I'll be right over."

"No! Not here! Meet me in the cemetery a little after eleven. I've got a piano lesson first."

"Okay. I'll be there."

Lynn hung up and went back out to the kitchen. The egg lay motionless in the skillet, looking up at her with its big yellow eye. It looked dead. Everything looked dead—the trees, the grass, the sky. It was a good month for dying.

Silently she ate her toast, staring out the window at

the meadow and the creek beyond, and wondered what Marjorie had to tell her. She was prepared for anything. Anything at all could happen, and she wouldn't be surprised. Everything was building toward a climax. When it came, and she or Mouse or both were bodily transfigured or transported or whatever by Mrs. Tuggle, the Beasleys and the Morleys would get together and weep and wonder why they had never believed the girls in the first place.

Thinking about it filled her eyes with tears, and she snuffed loudly. What was it that adults found so hard to accept? Father believed that absolutely everything could be explained in scientific terms. Mother at least said she believed that there were many things science knew nothing about, but witchcraft didn't seem to be one of them. Why was everyone so afraid even to consider it? Just because it had never happened before in this town—that they knew of, anyway—didn't mean it couldn't happen now.

And what did they really know about Mrs. Tuggle? That she and her husband built the house up on the hill and that Mr. Tuggle had run his small farm until he died fifteen years ago. That Mrs. Tuggle's young brother had drowned forty years ago. That was all. Everybody knew who Mrs. Tuggle was; everyone said hello when they met on the street; but no one really knew her well. No one. For a woman who had lived here most of her life, she certainly hadn't gone out of her way to make friends.

And then Mother had taken a walk up there one day, looking for a room to rent as a studio, and had fallen in love with Mrs. Tuggle's hen house. (It was all those nesting boxes along the back wall, she said.) Mrs. Tuggle had helped her clean and remodel it; and then—bit by bit—the old woman had crept into the Morley household by teaching Judith to sew.

"You want us to burn her at the stake for that?" Father had asked when Lynn told him about the crows and the way Mrs. Tuggle talked to them. What would her parents have thought if they had been along the day Lynn accused her of witchcraft? If they had seen her down by the creek themselves, with the nine crows on her outstretched arms? If they had seen the look in her eyes as she strode toward the creek the day that Mouse fell in? Could anyone really say she was normal?

Perhaps not, Lynn was sure her mother would say. *Perhaps the old dear is a little daft in some ways. But that doesn't make her a witch, does it?*

Lynn stood up and dumped her dishes in the sink. Then she trotted upstairs to change into jeans and a jacket. As she passed her parents' bedroom on the second floor, Mrs. Morley came out, one finger to her lips.

"Be extra quiet this morning, Lynn," she said. "Your

129

father didn't sleep well and feels as though he has a fever. It must be the flu."

Lynn nodded and went on up to her bedroom on the top floor, where Judith's breathing came steadily from behind the curtain. She collected all her clothes and took them down to the living room so she could dress near the hot air register. Ten-thirty. By now Mouse would be at her music lesson. She got the comics section from the newspaper, lay down on the rug and read them twice. Then, unable to concentrate on anything else, she put on her jacket, gloves, and a crocheted cap over her ears, and set out through the garden toward the creek below and the cemetery beyond. The crows were nowhere in sight.

She crossed the footbridge at the bottom of the meadow and then started up the steep hill of the old cemetery on the other side. The ground was frozen now, and instead of the soft crunch of yellow-brown autumn grass underfoot, the earth had a crisp, crackling sound. The branches of the sycamore trees waved stark and bare against the gray sky, and Lynn wished she had worn a heavy scarf around her neck, partly to keep out the wind, partly as protection should the crows attack her again. Somehow she did not think they would—not as long as Mouse was with her, as long as Mouse wore the ring. She wondered suddenly if that was it, if Mouse had lost the ring. What if they were meeting way out here without any protection at all?

She walked quickly through the gates that hung askew and on up to the grave of Mrs. Elfreda Lewis, where she sat down on the fallen tombstone.

The sound of crows came from somewhere in the distance, growing louder little by little, until finally Lynn could see them in the trees beyond. She knew that Mouse was coming, and leaned back to wait, her eyes on the two white marble angels across from her, over the grave of C. L. Pritchard. Sometimes, when Lynn looked at them, she was sure that one of them smiled, very slightly, just a slight curl of the lip, but she refused to believe it herself. Today the angels did not smile. They looked down with lidless eyes at the scroll they held between them and waited for Mouse to arrive.

In a few minutes, the squeak of Marjorie's bicycle sounded at the other gate facing the street, followed by a clunk of metal as Mouse dumped her bike and headed across the graveyard on foot. She was still clutching her sheet music from the piano lesson. Her hair was wild and windblown, and she wore her father's old army jacket over jeans. But as soon as Lynn saw her face, she forgot all about how Marjorie looked. Mouse sank down on the ground beside her with wide, terrified eyes.

"Lynn, the most awful thing has happened! Mrs.

Tuggle stopped by the bookstore yesterday and got talking with Daddy, and she told him how much she likes me and said how lonely she gets up there and everything, and what happened is that Daddy wants me to go up and stay with her tonight when he goes to a book auction in New York. He already told her I'd come!"

Lynn stared, and she was sure that her heart had stopped beating. Absolutely stopped! How *could* he? How wrong they had been not to tell him about Mrs. Tuggle earlier. He would never listen to them now! But would he ever have believed them? When he hadn't even believed about the crows?

She could not talk. She felt she could not even breathe. Her thoughts were smothered, as though her brain was paralyzed. And then she heard a sound that she thought was someone laughing, coming from somewhere up above. When she looked up, all she could see were the nine black crows. But then, through the tangle of gray branches, she made out the form of a cat.

chapter seven

It was all up to her now, Lynn knew. She could not ask Mr. Beasley to change his mind; he was already upset with her. That was clear. Always before, it would have just been assumed that Mouse would stay with the Morleys. But not this time.

She could hardly call Mrs. Beasley long distance and ask her to come back. She could not tell her own parents and risk a quarrel between them again, especially when they would not believe her anyway. For a moment she thought of Judith. At least it would be three girls, not two, against Mrs. Tuggle. But she decided against that also. Now that Judith had broken off with the old woman and remembered little of what had gone on, it was better not to involve her again.

Lynn drew her knees up and hugged them to her to stop the shaking. She was more frightened than if she, herself, were going to Mrs. Tuggle's for the night. At least then she would know what was going on because she would be there. But how could she protect Marjorie? Being responsible for her friend made the terror all the greater. Mouse would not be able to hold out against the power of the evil woman. She was weakening already. Even now, she looked like a pile of old clothes crumpled in a heap on the ground.

"All right, Mouse, I've got it," Lynn said suddenly, grabbing Mouse firmly by the arm to show that she was strong. "Go back home and pretend that things are fine. *Smile*, Mouse. Be cheerful even if it kills you. No, I didn't mean that. But act perfectly natural. Pack your things as though you're going to Mrs. Tuggle's. What time's your father leaving?"

"Two o'clock. His flight is at three."

"And when are you supposed to go to Mrs. Tuggle's?"

"Six—in time for dinner."

"Great. The minute your father leaves, bring your stuff over to our house. You'll stay all night with us instead."

"I *asked* him if I could go to your house, Lynn, and he said I'd imposed on your family enough, and that Mrs. Tuggle was lonely and would be glad to have me."

"She'd be delighted to eat you, Mouse! And you

haven't imposed on us at all. You're going to come."

"What will I tell Mrs. Tuggle?"

"Nothing. I'll call her later and say that there's been a change in plans."

"But what if Daddy finds out?"

"He won't till it's all over—if then. You'll just have to tell him that you're terrified of her, that's all. It's better than having him come back from New York to find out you've disappeared altogether."

Marjorie swallowed audibly.

"But *don't* tell him before he leaves, Mouse. If Mrs. Tuggle calls, tell her you'll be there at six. You've got to put on a good act. You've got to pretend you're not scared."

"Lynn, it'll never work."

"*Why* won't it work?"

"Because . . . she'll come after me. I know it."

"She won't know a thing till you're safe in our house," Lynn promised. "Now go on home, Mouse, and act as if everything's okay."

Marjorie went back through the cemetery the way she had come, and Lynn heard the squeak of her bike as she got on it at the west entrance and rode back out to the street. The crows left with her, cawing and bickering among themselves, but the cat remained in the tree, watching without moving. Lynn got up and started home at a run, then remembered and slowed down. It was important that she remain calm too, that she give no hint that anything was wrong.

She went up the hill through the garden and in the back door. Mother was at the stove making coffee.

"Mom," Lynn said casually, taking a slice of bread for herself and spreading it with honey. "Mouse is coming over to spend the night. Okay?"

Mrs. Morley turned around. "Oh, not *tonight*, Lynn! Your father's sick with the flu, and now Stevie's vomiting. We're probably all going to be in for a rough weekend. Maybe next Saturday she can but not tonight."

Lynn's heart sank to her feet. She had been so sure of her plan.

"But . . . but we'll be sleeping way upstairs. We won't bother anyone. . . ."

"Not *tonight*, Lynn! It wouldn't be fair to Marjorie to expose her to our germs. And with everyone wanting the bathroom at once, it's no fun having a guest in the house. No, she absolutely can't stay here tonight." Mother poured a cup of coffee, put it on a tray with a glass of orange juice, and took it upstairs for Father.

Lynn sank down on a chair. What on earth would she do now? What would she tell Mouse? How could things possibly turn out so horribly? Tears came to her eyes, tears for her friend, but they receded as soon as she heard her mother's footsteps on the stairs again. It was important not to seem upset so that no one would ask questions. She remembered the bread she hadn't touched and took a bite.

"Well, can I go to Marjorie's then for the night? I feel great, and I don't particularly want to be here either if everyone's throwing up."

"It's all right with me if Mr. Beasley says you may," Mother answered.

"Okay, then. I'll go over around two and be home tomorrow sometime."

Lynn felt a flood of relief as she took her bread into the music room and ate it on the window seat. It was several minutes before her heart stopped pounding.

At one-thirty, she stuffed her pajamas, toothbrush and underwear in a sack and went to the other side of the bedroom to talk with Judith a few minutes. Then she drew a silly picture for Stevie to cheer him up, looked in on her father, said good-bye to Mother, and went out the front door.

She realized, as she started down the hill, that she had said good-bye to her family as though she might never see them again. She shook her head quickly to clear it of the thought. She had purposely tried not to think of her and Mouse alone all night, and she certainly wasn't going to start thinking scary thoughts now.

A taxi was already sitting out in front of the Beasley house. Lynn sat down on a stone wall, hidden by a large bush, and waited.

A minute passed, then two. What if Mrs. Tuggle had called and Mouse had lost her nerve and told her father everything? The crows in the large oak tree behind the house seemed agitated and fussed about in the branches, pecking occasionally at each other and cawing loudly. Then the door opened, and the crows fell silent. Mr. Beasley stepped out on the porch with his suitcase, said something to Mouse there in the doorway, leaned down and kissed her, talked some more, and left. Lynn waited till the taxi was out of sight before she stood up and ran to the house.

This time the crows rose up on their talons and shrieked loudly, and the lead crow flew down to the roof of the porch. But a moment later Lynn was knocking on the door, and Mouse let her in.

"Lynn! I was just about to come over," Mouse said, surprised.

"There's been a change in plans." Lynn took off her coat and dropped her sack on the floor. "I'm staying here all night instead. Dad and Stevie have the flu, and Mother's afraid the whole family is coming down with it, so she said I could stay here instead."

Mouse stared. "All by ourselves? Does she know that Daddy? . . ."

"No," Lynn said. "She doesn't."

Mouse slid down against the wall till she was sitting on the floor, legs sprawled out in front of her. "What if Mrs. Tuggle calls your folks and tells them that we're here alone?"

"Well, first of all, I'm not going to tell Mrs. Tuggle that. I'm just going to say that there's been a change in plans, and that you're to spend the night with me instead."

"But—"

"I didn't say *where*, did I?"

"What if she calls your mother and complains, and says that my father told her I'd be staying with her?"

"I'll tell Mother that your father got uneasy about it and changed his mind just before he left."

"What if Mrs. Tuggle calls Daddy in New York?"

That was something Lynn had not thought of.

"Does she know where he's staying?"

A half-smile crossed Marjorie's face. "No," she said and pointed to a slip of paper on a stand near the door. "That's his phone number, and I was supposed to give it to her when I went up to her house."

"Great!" said Lynn. "Then it's all settled." She walked on into the living room and put her things on a chair. "Mouse . . . you still . . . uh . . . you're still wearing that ring, aren't you?"

"Yes. . . ."

"Well, don't take it off tonight. I mean, especially tonight. . . ."

They decided not to call Mrs. Tuggle until almost six o'clock. The less time the old woman had to think about revenge, the better. Lynn concentrated on keeping Mouse occupied; on making the afternoon seem as normal as possible. They got out the Monopoly set and played until Mouse had built hotels on both Boardwalk and Park Place. They changed the water in the aquarium, made milkshakes, looked through Marjorie's scrapbooks, played "Chopsticks" on the piano, listened to records, and practiced headstands.

At five o'clock someone rang the doorbell. Mouse collapsed on the rug where she was doing push-ups and looked at Lynn.

"Don't answer," Lynn whispered, motionless.

"But we ought to just see who it is," Mouse protested. She crawled over to the window and peeped out from behind the drapes.

"It's only the paperboy," she said, relieved. "Dad left some money to pay him."

She ran upstairs, returned with the three dollars, and opened the door. It was then that the girls noticed the huge black crow perched on the top of the lattice, which extended halfway up one side of the porch.

"That your pet?" the newsboy asked, as he took the

money and gave them a stub in return.

"N . . . No," Mouse stammered. "He doesn't belong to us."

"Oh. I thought he did. I noticed him sitting there when I was collecting on the other side of the street. And he's still sitting there."

Lynn came to the door. Was it possible that the crows were getting bolder now—that they wouldn't fly away if others noticed? Maybe they could use the paperboy as a witness if no one else would believe them. . . .

"Doesn't it seem strange that a crow would just hang around like this when we don't feed it or anything?" she asked him.

"Nope. You can make a pet out of most anything if you try."

"But we haven't tried."

The boy shrugged. "Somebody probably has. Probably someone's pet that got away. Well, see you next month," he said and went back down the steps whistling.

Did he see the eight other crows in the tree by the side of the house, Lynn wondered. Wouldn't he think it sort of unusual? But the paperboy didn't even look at the trees, and soon he had disappeared around the corner. The crow sat motionless, its eyes on Mouse.

Marjorie quickly closed the door, leaning heavily against it.

"Nevermore," she said.

Lynn stared. "What?"

Mouse seemed to be in a trance. She didn't move, but stood with her eyes wide:

> *"Once upon a midnight dreary, while*
> *I pondered weak and weary,*
> *Over many a quaint and curious volume*
> *of forgotten lore—*
> *While I nodded, nearly napping,*
> *suddenly there came a tapping,*
> *As of some one gently rapping, rapping*
> *at my chamber door. . . .*

Lynn pulled her away from the door. "Mouse, what's got into you?"

"Don't you know it, Lynn? That poem by Edgar Allan Poe about a raven that got into a man's house and wouldn't leave, and all it would ever say was 'nevermore'?"

Now that she mentioned it, Lynn did remember, but she wished she hadn't.

"Daddy used to read it to me sometimes," Mouse said, getting a book down from a shelf. She turned to the poem and laid it on Lynn's lap. "What if that's the raven, Lynn? I mean, what if it stays forever? If it does, I'll go crazy, you know."

"Good grief, Mouse! That bird's out there, not in here, and if it's still there when your Dad comes back, let him worry about it. Then he'll know we're not imagining things. Poe was great at scaring people to death."

But it made her uneasy, nonetheless, having the bird so close and so bold now, and as her eyes quickly scanned the poem, the last verse sent shivers through her:

> And the Raven, never flitting, still is
>   sitting, still is sitting
> On the pallid bust of Pallas, just
>   above my chamber door;
> And his eyes have all the seeming of
>   a demon that is dreaming,
> And the lamplight o'er him streaming
>   throws his shadow on the floor;
> And my soul from out that shadow
>   that lies floating on the floor
> Shall be lifted—nevermore!

She slammed the book shut suddenly, angry at herself for reading it.

"Okay, Mouse, just to make you feel better, we're going through this whole house and lock every window and door. We won't just close them; we'll be sure they're locked tightly. Then we can stop worrying."

Still pale, Mouse nodded and went up to the bedrooms above. Lynn checked the downstairs. The sun was getting low in the sky, and she knew it would soon be time to call Mrs. Tuggle. The crow, on the lattice, was still there.

At five-thirty, she sat down by the telephone in the Beasley kitchen and dialed. Mouse stood with her back against the refrigerator, her face grim. Lynn heard the phone ringing at the other end. One . . . two . . . three rings, and then an old woman's wavering voice saying, "Yes?"

"Mrs. Tuggle, this is Lynn Morley," Lynn said sounding as businesslike as she could. "I'm calling to tell you that there has been a change in plans, and Marjorie won't be staying with you this evening. She's staying with me instead."

Lynn had planned to say only that, end it with "goodbye," and hang up. But she just couldn't do it. Even with Mrs. Tuggle, it sounded far too impolite.

There was silence at the other end. Absolute quiet. Lynn squirmed. She hadn't expected this. She wished that Mrs. Tuggle would say something.

"We . . . just thought you might want to know so you wouldn't go to any extra trouble," she added finally.

And then, from the other end of the line came a low, rapid recitation that Lynn could not understand—an angry chant of nonsense words, or perhaps it was Greek, she didn't know. Louder and faster the voice went, and now and then Lynn recognized her own name in the chant.

It sounded so horrible, so completely terrifying, that Lynn slammed down the receiver quickly.

"What *happened?*" Mouse asked, frantic. "What did she say? Lynn, you're white!"

Lynn sat back on the stool and gripped the edges with her fingers. "She's furious, Mouse. I just knew she'd be. Now I'll bet she calls my mother and tells her. Mom will call here and insist that I come back, and . . . Mouse, if they say you've got to go to Mrs. Tuggle's, we'll run away. We'll hide out at the bus station all night or something."

She began to feel sick, and her knees wobbled. Maybe she was getting the flu.

"I think I'd better lie down, Mouse," she said, and went in to the sofa. Marjorie followed and sat beside her, both of them waiting for the phone to ring. But it did not. Occasionally they pulled aside the drapes and looked out, half expecting either Mrs. Tuggle or the Morleys. But no one came. The crow on the lattice kept a silent vigil. The sun went down, and the room began to grow dark. Mrs. Tuggle must not have called the Morleys after all.

Lynn began to feel better and was ashamed of being so shaky. If anything could scare Mouse to death, it

145

was sitting around like this in the dark waiting for something awful to happen.

"I'm hungry," she said, getting up and turning on a lamp. "What have we got for dinner, Mouse?"

"Shredded wheat," said Marjorie.

"What?"

"It's what I had for breakfast," Mouse said. "I didn't know you were coming for dinner."

They went out in the kitchen and rummaged through the refrigerator.

"How about grilled cheese sandwiches with sweet pickles?" Mouse said finally, "and here's some tuna from yesterday."

"Great," said Lynn. "That's all we need."

They turned on the radio and set to work buttering the bread and toasting it on a skillet. The music made them feel far less alone. After they had eaten, they stuck marshmallows on long-handled forks and browned them on the flame of the gas stove. By the time the meal was over, they were feeling considerably better. If Mrs. Tuggle was going to report to Lynn's parents, she would certainly have done so by now. She undoubtedly assumed that Mouse was at the Morleys. Still, the crow. . . .

They took a bowl of crackers into the living room and turned on the TV. For an hour they sat watching a CBS special on India until they finally decided they weren't that interested and turned it off. Mouse yawned and looked at the clock. Nine-thirty.

"I'm tired," she said. "I want to go to bed."

"Already? It's not even ten!"

"I know, but I'm all scared out."

Lynn laughed. "Okay. Let's get in bed and talk awhile."

Both of them wanted to look out and see if the crow was still there, but neither admitted it. So they checked the front and back doors once more to be sure they were locked, turned out the lights, and went upstairs to Marjorie's room. There was a faint scratching sound at the window, and both girls jumped when they heard it, but it was only a branch from the oak tree, rubbing against the pane. They laughed, put on their pajamas, and dived between the sheets, their icy toes touching beneath the covers.

Mouse fell asleep at once, but Lynn knew she could not possibly sleep with midnight yet to come. Somewhere she had heard that a witch's power is greatest at twelve o'clock, and she could not afford to take chances. She had hoped Mouse would stay awake to keep her company, but Marjorie lay motionless except for an occasional twitch of an arm or leg. A few minutes later she was actually snoring, and Lynn smiled in the darkness. Too bad she didn't have a tape recorder so she could play it back tomorrow at breakfast.

It was very quiet in the Beasley house, more quiet than at home. There were no muffled sounds of people walking around downstairs or of Judith turning pages on the other side of the curtain. The furnace didn't squeak as it did at Lynn's, and because there was more yard space around Marjorie's home, neighbors and their noises were farther away. Only the wind seemed stronger here, which was strange because the house was located further downhill. Perhaps, because there were no storm windows, it was easier for the wind to work through the cracks and crevices and to whistle around the panes—a hypnotic sound that rose and fell as the sky grew blacker.

Things seemed so safe and secure here under the blankets, the night so normal. Lynn thought about her own family. Mother was probably going back and forth between her bedroom and Stevie's, taking temperatures and pouring orange juice and rubbing Father's back. Judith was probably up in the bedroom listening to records. Lynn even thought of Mrs. Tuggle and for a moment felt a slight wave of remorse. What if the old woman were merely crazy and had meant no harm at all? What if she had gone to a lot of trouble to prepare a good dinner for Marjorie? Then Lynn remembered the way she had looked down at the creek the day Mouse fell in and the strange words she had uttered over the phone. She remembered the crows in the trees outside—waiting. It was still a long time before midnight.

At eleven she got up to go to the bathroom, went downstairs for another marshmallow and a glass of milk, checked the doors again to make sure that they were locked, and went back to bed. Mouse was sleeping so soundly she hadn't even changed position.

Lynn rolled her pillow up under her head and pulled the blankets up under her chin. What was it like, she wondered, to be Marjorie, to sleep in this room every night, to have a father who sold books and a mother who lived in Ohio? What was it like to be a girl with short brown hair and big glasses, a pug nose and skinny legs, who took piano lessons on Saturdays and spent half her life in a purple poncho? How strange it was, when she really thought about it, that she could never be anyone else, even for a moment . . . that she would never know for sure what it was like to be Marjorie. She was a prisoner of her own body and could never get outside it, ever. Unless, of course, she were bodily transfigured by witchcraft. . . .

She was conscious of the wind getting louder now, strangely stronger than it had seemed before, and suddenly she sat straight up, clutching the blanket to her throat. It was not just the whistle of the wind that had caught her attention. It was a tune, borne on the wind . . . or did she just imagine it? She listened again, her eyes wide, holding her breath so that not even the slightest sound would distract her. There it was again . . . she was sure of it . . . the tune that Mrs. Tuggle had sung the day that she and Mouse had paid her a visit:

> Sing of morning, sing of noon,
> Sing of evening's silver moon,
> Feel the darkness, touch the black,
> Hear the shadows whisper back.

Lynn felt the fine hair on her arms stand straight up as though her very skin were rising. It *must* be her imagination. *Nobody* could make the wind do its bidding, not even Mrs. Tuggle. But the melody continued, even stronger than before, even though Lynn clamped her hands over her ears. And this time the words themselves came through, as if Mrs. Tuggle were there in the room singing them herself:

> Feel the darkness, touch the black,
> Hear the shadows whisper back.

Lynn reached out quickly and turned on the lamp beside the bed. Was she going mad? Hearing voices; wasn't that one of the signs? There was only one way to find out. She shook Mouse.

"Mouse, I think you'd better wake up."

"Hmmmmmmph."

"Mouse, please wake up! I think . . . I think something's happening. . . ."

Marjorie rolled over, her eyelids half-open, and suddenly she was asleep again.

This time Lynn shook her till her head rolled back and forth on the pillow. "Mouse, you've got to stay awake! I need you!"

Mouse lifted her head, looked at Lynn, and finally raised up on one elbow, locks of hair hanging down over her face. "What time is it?"

"A quarter of twelve."

Mouse sat up. "Who's singing?"

"Then you *do* hear it!" Lynn gasped. "I was afraid I was going nuts! What does it sound like?"

"M . . . Mrs. Tuggle!" Mouse choked and grabbed at Lynn as though she were drowning.

Lynn shook her again. "Listen, Mouse, we're okay. I checked all the doors again! No one can get in. It's important not to let her scare us."

They stopped talking and listened again to see if they could still hear it. Yes, there it was—as distinct now as if the old woman were standing beside the bed whispering it to them. Their own shadows on the wall opposite were huge and terrible in the light of the lamp.

"What should we d . . . do?" Mouse whispered.

"Sing with it!" Lynn said determinedly. "Then she'll know we're not afraid. *Sing of morning, sing of noon, sing of evening's silver moon.* . . . Come on, Mouse, join in! As loud as you can! *Feel the darkness, touch the black. . . .*" Their voices rose to a yell. *"Hear the shadows whisper back!"*

When they had finished the song, they stopped and listened again. Only the wind remained.

"See?" Lynn cried excitedly. "We can beat her at her own game, Mouse! The most she can do is scare us!"

Something caught her eye outside the window, however—a gleam, a sparkle of light, something that had not been there before. Mouse saw it too.

"Lynn . . ." she whispered.

Lynn turned out the lamp so they could see more clearly and together they crept out of bed and over the cold floor to the window.

Two yellow eyes stared in, and the huge form of Mrs. Tuggle's cat was silhouetted against the moon, sitting on the branch of the oak tree, its tail swishing rhythmically like the pendulum of a clock ticking off the minutes till midnight.

"It can't get in," Lynn said reassuringly, but as she stared out the window, her eyes growing accustomed to the darkness, she could make out the forms of crows in the tree outside—not just nine, but dozens—silent black bodies—a hundred, maybe—sitting motionless, waiting. . . .

She pulled Mouse away from the window so she would not notice them too. "Let's go downstairs and make some hot chocolate," she suggested. They pulled on their socks, wrapped themselves in blankets, and went down to the kitchen.

The moment Lynn reached the kitchen doorway, however, before she turned on the light, she could see them out the window in the moonlight: cats. Dozens of cats. They were sitting on the branches, on the fence, the tool shed, and they all sat motionless like the crows, faces turned toward the house . . . all waiting. . . .

What on earth did it mean? What were they going to do?

It was all part of Mrs. Tuggle's plan to wear her and Mouse down by keeping them terrified, she was sure of it. Her heart pounded as she quickly turned on the light and pulled down the shade. It was ten minutes till midnight.

"Where's the cocoa?" she asked and noticed the tremor in her own voice.

Marjorie climbed up on a chair and got it down from the cupboard. Lynn measured some into a pan and added milk.

There was a scratching noise outside the window.

"What's that?" Mouse said, whirling around.

"Just a branch or something," Lynn said. "Get the sugar, Mouse."

But Marjorie stood in the middle of the floor, her eyes on the window, the blanket sliding down off her shoulders.

"That's not the wind, Lynn, it's something else," she said and walked over to the window.

"Don't open the shade," Lynn cautioned, but it was too late. Six or seven cats were on the sill outside, all meowing and scratching at the glass, their snarling mouths open, faces almost human in the light from the kitchen.

Mouse screamed. She backed away from the window, her screaming becoming more and more hysterical. She dashed into the living room, Lynn after her, but the windows there seemed to be crawling with crows—huge black birds with large, outstretched wings, flapping about and attacking the glass with their beaks. Mouse rolled into a corner, arms around her head, screaming wildly.

Lynn threw herself on Mouse as though to protect her and huddled against the wall with her arms around her, as from all directions now the meowing of the cats and the screech of the crows grew louder and louder. The birds had begun attacking the glass now, flinging against it with their bodies, thudding hard against the pane, like demons wild to get in. They *were* demons,

Lynn was sure of it, controlled by Mrs. Tuggle and destined to do her bidding: to bring the girls to her or to drive them mad.

"I can't stand it, Lynn!" Mouse screamed. "I've got to get out of here! I'll tell her I'll do anything if she'll just keep the crows away. I can't stand it, I'm going to Mrs. Tuggle's! Lynn, I can't stand it!" she struggled to get up.

Lynn wrestled her down and pinned her hard against the rug.

"You're *not* going, Mouse!" Lynn choked, half-crying. "You're *strong*, Mouse! Stronger than you think! Our friendship is stronger than you think! Our friendship is stronger than anything!" she screamed, for Mrs. Tuggle to hear. "Stronger than witchcraft!"

She held Marjorie down with all her might, but just then the clock began the long slow count of midnight, and suddenly there was a scrambling, fluttering noise that seemed to come from inside the walls.

"The chimney!" Mouse screamed.

chapter eight

Terror rose up in Lynn so swiftly that it cut off her breath. She had locked and checked every door and window in the house, but the fireplace flue was open, and something was coming down. Outside the cats and crows shrieked like a jungle of demented spirits.

"Close it!" Lynn screamed, springing up on her knees, but Marjorie could not move.

Tumbling across the rug, Lynn rolled toward the fireplace, every muscle, every nerve alive with one intention only. In another two seconds the first crow or cat would have clawed its way into the living room through the open chimney, and would be followed by dozens more.

As her knee hit the stone hearth, her arm was already reaching up for the iron handle that operated the flue. Her fingers gripped it, feeling the cool air that was rushing down from above, just as a huge black wing appeared from out the dark hole.

Wham! With a clang the heavy iron trap door came down, and Lynn reeled backwards, weak with fright. For a full minute she did not move. The pounding of her heart was so great that it seemed to pin her to the floor. Gradually the beating grew slower, and feeling returned to her legs. She sat up and looked at Mouse and then at the fireplace.

Caught in the heavy trap door of the flue was the body of the lead crow. One wing and the head were inside the room, and the yellow eyes, once so sharp and menacing, were glazed over now. The wing twitched once and hung motionless. And then Lynn realized that the noise outside had stopped.

"Mouse," she whispered. "Listen."

Together they crouched on opposite sides of the room, absolutely still, listening. But the demon sounds were gone.

They crept across the rug to the window and peered out. The trees were bare. There were no birds silhouetted against the moon, no gleaming eyes, no sounds of scratching and clawing, no meowing. The night was still, as nights should be.

"We did it!" Lynn said, half squealing, half crying. "Oh, Mouse! We did it! The lead crow is dead. We broke the spell!"

The girls leaped up, clutching at each other, and whirled about the room in a giddy display of confidence and power. Finally they collapsed in an exhausted heap, still dazed by the events of the evening.

Mouse leaned back against the wall. "What would they have done, Lynn, if they'd got in?"

Lynn shuddered. "I don't know. I don't know if Mrs. Tuggle wants us dead or alive right now. But we're *strong*, Mouse! We *did* it! She can't hurt us now!"

"What should we do with the crow?"

"Let's just leave it. Show it to your father. But don't be surprised if he doesn't believe you, Mouse. He'll say that anybody can get a crow in the chimney."

Up in the bedroom, the girls lay on their backs looking sleepily out the window, which had held such horror for them only minutes ago.

"You were right," Mouse murmured, "about our friendship. About it being stronger than anything, Lynn."

"You've got a whole new start now, Mouse," Lynn told her. "You can go wherever you want without the crows coming along. You can look Mrs. Tuggle right in the eye if you meet her on the street because she knows you're strong. Everybody will notice and wonder what's happened to you, but we won't tell. What happened here tonight will be our secret, until our parents are ready to listen and believe us."

For some reason the idea appealed to Mouse. It was great to be somebody special—somebody snatched from the jaws of witchcraft, even. "I might even wash my hair," she mused, "if I can find the shampoo. Listen, Lynn, don't wake me in the morning. I feel I could sleep till noon."

Lynn had expected to sleep late also. She had expected, at the very least, that her sleep would be deep and relaxed; but when she woke at seven-thirty, she knew she would sleep no more. Somehow she felt uneasy, as if the trouble was not quite over, as if there was something left undone. She felt that her mind had been wrestling with it as she slept; and now that it was morning, she remembered suddenly what it was and what she must do. She felt strong and unfrightened as she dressed quietly and went downstairs.

Mouse, she wrote in a note which she left on the table. *Out for a walk. Back about eleven, Lynn.*

She knew, from the deep sleep Marjorie was in, that it would be several hours at least before she found the note. And that would give Lynn time for the task before her.

As she started down the steps and across the lawn, she stopped, for the ground was littered with blue-black feathers. Should she pick them up, she wondered, and deliver them knowingly to Mrs. Tuggle? No, she would leave them where they were for evidence, for whatever Mr. Beasley cared to make of it when he got back from New York.

The streets were empty. The sky in the east was bright, but everywhere shades were still drawn and curtains closed. Lynn went quickly across the meadow. An early morning mist was rising from the water, and the whole of Cowden's Creek seemed veiled in fog. Her pulse quickened as she started down the hill to the water below. It was not enough to have saved Mouse from Mrs. Tuggle's coven, whatever it was the old woman needed her for. It was not enough that Judith had escaped her influence, and that Stevie was safe, or that the crows would no longer trail Marjorie. It was important that the evil of the night before should never be allowed to begin again, at some distant time in the future. And this, she had decided, meant killing the demon cat.

The cat, Lynn knew, roamed about the neighborhood at will. Many mornings Lynn had looked out the bathroom window and seen it making its way up through the meadow from the creek below. She would lie in wait for the cat. How she would confront it, much less kill it, she did not know. She didn't even want to think about it for fear she would change her mind. All she could do was rely on her strength and intuition when the time came.

The fog grew thicker the closer she got to the water, and by the time she reached the bank of Cowden's Creek, the fog was a swirling mass of whiteness covering the surface of the water, which seemed strangely churned up, hissing and rushing as it poured under the footbridge.

Lynn sat down on the bank to wait. She had a better chance of finding the cat, she decided, if she let it come to her than if she went looking for it. The ground was cold and rather damp, and she wished she had brought a newspaper to sit on. There were no early morning sounds of birds, no raucous chants of crows. Only the rush of water from the creek and the moving mist, which seemed, in some strange way, to be making a sound of its own.

She was not sure how long she waited—twenty minutes, maybe—perhaps thirty. But then, at the far end of the footbridge, she saw a dark brown object coming toward her in the fog, one paw in front of the other, stopping now and then to sniff the air.

Slowly Lynn stood up and started on down the bank. She had brought no weapons but her own two hands, and somehow she knew she would choke the cat with them. Yet she had never killed anything in her life, unless you counted ants stepped on accidentally or a mosquito now and then or the lightning bug she had once held too tightly in her hands. There was no doubt in her mind, however, that the cat had to go, and that she must be the one to kill it. To use her own two hands was to destroy forever any link she, herself, may have had with Mrs. Tuggle—whatever excitement or fascination she may have felt in the past when she thought of witchcraft. To bury the cat there on the banks of Cowden's Creek would be to bury along with it any talent of her own she may have gleaned from reading the Beasley book on spells and potions. Once she, herself, was free from the spell of witchcraft, she knew that Mrs. Tuggle's magic would have an effect on her no longer. And so she stepped onto the end of the footbridge and saw the cat pause.

They stood there looking at each other along the expanse of wood planking as the mist drifted in and out between them, sometimes clouding their view, sometimes revealing each other sharp and clear.

Lynn half expected the cat to say something, to warn her not to come closer, but the animal stood still, waiting, his eyes on Lynn, a look of evil about him—a smell, an aura of evil—that Lynn could not describe. Step by step she advanced, her arms aching with tension, lips dry, eyes on the huge cat.

And then it sprang. There was a blur of a brown body as it propelled itself through the air and landed hard on Lynn's shoulder, knocking her to the floor of the bridge. With all her strength, Lynn seized the cat, oblivious to the bites and scratches, and a moment later they had rolled under the guard rail, into the churning shallow water below.

Lynn landed on her side, and for a moment the air seemed to have been knocked out of her. Her face went under momentarily, then emerged, but she clung to the cat and the cat to her. She had never known an animal could be so strong. It was like wrestling with Stevie, almost. Like a whip, the cat's body flung back and forth, its claws scratching her arms, its teeth digging in her shoulder, a hideous yowling in its throat. Lynn's one aim was to work her hands up the cat's body to its neck, but she knew if she let go for even an instant, the cat would get away. She would have to drown it instead.

The creek was livid with splashing and thrashing as cat and girl fought there in the water. Lynn's knees were bruised as she battered them against the rocks on the bottom. Her whole body was cold—almost stiff. Again the cat surfaced and shrieked, and again they tumbled over and over. But as Lynn righted herself a third time, she managed to thrust the cat under her and hold it down under the water with all her strength.

Lynn held the cat until the current tugged it out of her tired arms, rolling her over. She didn't care. She had felt the squirming body grow limp, and knew that the deed was done. Slowly she crawled across the rocky bottom of the creek to the bank and lay there shivering, completely exhausted, strangely weak. She realized that now she as well as Mouse had been bathed in the spell of the creek, whatever that meant. Perhaps it meant nothing. Now that the lead crow and the cat were dead, perhaps the rushing water had lost whatever power it had held. When she had the strength to sit up and look at it, it did seem more like the lazy old Cowden's Creek that it had been once. At least she thought it did.

Suddenly she felt like shouting. She felt like standing up on the bank, lifting her face to the sky, and giving a wild jubilant yell. She felt like dancing, like rolling over and over and over on the grass, laughing and singing. She had finally outwitted the old woman and got rid of her demons as well. Lynn had never felt so happy.

It was too early in the morning for shouting, however. So she got to her feet and walked along the edge of the creek for a while, hugging herself with her arms, looking for the body of the cat, numb with the cold. She had wanted to bury it deep in the ground, but the current had washed it away. No matter. It would be floating down toward the business district by now, and Lynn was too weary to go after it. So she headed up through the meadow to her house, rehearsing what she was going to say.

Through the kitchen window she could see the clock on the wall. Ten after nine. Father was sitting at the table alone reading the Sunday paper. She opened the back door and stepped inside.

"Ye gods! What happened to *you*?" Mr. Morley paused with his coffee cup in midair.

Lynn laughed blithely. "I went for a walk down by the creek, leaned too far over the footbridge and fell in. I came home to change."

Mr. Morley continued to stare. "You look as if you had a fight with a tiger and lost."

"No tiger," Lynn said. "But those rocks in the creek are sharp, and the bushes along the bank can really scratch."

She started through the kitchen toward the stairs.

"I thought you were staying at Marjorie's."

"I was. She's still asleep. I just decided to get up early and go hiking. I'll go back and have breakfast with her after I change."

Still Father's eyes would not leave her. "You didn't have a fight with *Marjorie*, did you?"

Lynn laughed at the thought. "Now that's the most ridiculous thing *I* ever heard. Talk about imaginative nonsense."

"Well, Stevie had a pretty rough night, so go up quietly. We want him to sleep a long time."

Lynn tiptoed past the second floor and went on up

the stairs to her bedroom. As she was putting on dry jeans and a shirt—long-sleeved and high-necked to hide the scratches—she heard Judith roll over on the other side of the curtain.

"Lynn?"

"Yeah?"

"Gosh, I had the worst dream about you last night!"

Lynn buttoned her shirt and walked over to Judith's side of the bedroom. "What was it?"

Judith lay on her back and put her hands under her head. "Oh, it was all mixed up. You and Mouse were . . . in a boat or something. . . . Well, it was like a house, but it was in the water, sort of, and the water kept getting higher, and there were things floating in the water, awful things, but I don't know what they were. Maybe they were dead. I wanted to swim out and get you, but Mrs. Tuggle was there, and she wouldn't let me. . . ."

Lynn sat on the edge of the bed and waited.

"I can't remember any more," Judith said, finally. "It was just too awful. Once I called out your name in the night and you didn't answer, and finally I realized you were at Marjorie's. . . ." She sat up and propped her pillow behind her back. "I have this strange feeling sometimes—a scary feeling, but it's as though I've felt it before, only I can't remember when or where. Like, if I just thought about it long enough, I'd remember,

168

and all sorts of things would come back to me, but I'm not sure I want to. . . ."

"Don't even try," Lynn said hastily, remembering how worried she'd been last summer about Judith's going up to Mrs. Tuggle's house each night. "They're probably just old pieces of dreams, and you could spend a week trying to put them all together. Besides, Mouse and I are fine. I just came back home to get some clean clothes." She turned and walked over to the doorway. "I tell you what, Judith. If you're still having awful dreams when I'm a psychiatrist, I'll analyze them for you."

Judith laughed. "Then I'll go off the deep end for sure. Listen, is anyone up downstairs? I'm hungry."

"Dad is. Why don't you go down and scramble some eggs for him? He looks as if he could use it."

Lynn went back downstairs and got a handful of cookies from the kitchen cupboard. She was positive now she had done the right thing. Drowning the cat had meant breaking the link between Mrs. Tuggle and Judith, too. It was important that Judith never feel that strange pull, that demonic force, again.

"How are you feeling, Dad?" Lynn asked.

"Oh, better, I think."

"That's good." Lynn leaned against the counter. "By the way did the sheriff ever find out anything?"

"What?" Mr. Morley lowered his newspaper.

"About that missing death certificate."

"Oh. If he has, I haven't heard. It's only a routine check, Lynn. He could put it off for months. There's no hurry."

Lynn munched quietly. Mrs. Tuggle could do a lot in a few months, so that when the sheriff came snooping around, she'd be ready. If she had any power left, that is. . . . Now that the cat and the lead crow were gone, maybe she was finally what Mother and Father had insisted she was all along—a harmless old lady, a bit daft.

"Where's Mom?" Lynn asked.

"She went over to Mrs. Tuggle's to help out. There was evidently quite a wind up on the hill last night. Did you hear it? We didn't get much of it down here, but a tree blew down in Mrs. Tuggle's yard and tore off a small piece of the kitchen roof. She called this morning and told us. If my legs aren't too wobbly by afternoon, I'm going to go up and see if I can patch it up for her."

Lynn tried to sound casual. "Did she . . . did Mrs. Tuggle say anything else?"

"As a matter of fact, she asked if you children were safe—you, in particular. We said we assumed you were. I knew Mr. Beasley would have called us if you weren't."

Lynn's heart was in her mouth.

"And what did she say?"

"Good grief, Lynn, I don't know. I suppose she said, 'That's good' or something. What would you expect her to say?" He was beginning to look at her quizzically again, and Lynn knew it was time to stop asking questions.

"Well, I'm off," she said lightly. "When Mom comes home, tell her I'll be back this afternoon."

"Stay away from the creek, kid," Father called after her. "You're the only girl I know who can lean over the railing and fall in."

When Lynn reached the garden, however, she stopped. Mouse would still be sleeping, probably for another hour or two. Why not, right now while she was feeling strong, go up to Mrs. Tuggle's? She could say she had come to help out, that Dad had told her about the windstorm. But she would be showing Mrs. Tuggle that she wasn't afraid—that she could confront her even with Mother there. Let her dare tell Mother that she and Mouse had spent the night alone, and Lynn would have some telling of her own to do!

She chose the route along the edge of the meadow, making her way up the hill that rose steeper and steeper as she neared the top. On her right, she could see the mist from Cowden's Creek still rising in spotty patches here and there. Now and then a bird cut loose with an early morning trill—even a crow or two joined in. But the crows were scattered now—one here, one there—

and did not fly in a flock. The single crow she passed on the fence post went on preening itself disinterestedly and flew off languidly without a second look in her direction.

Lynn felt powerful and sure of herself—more sure than she had ever felt before. She and Marjorie were not just helpless victims who had to give in. They were more in control of their lives than they had thought. Witchcraft was not the strongest thing in the world. Friendship was even more powerful. Of course, killing the crow had helped. . . .

Mrs. Tuggle's house, from behind, looked quite different than it did from the front. Approaching the front door, one could hardly make out the porch because of the cluster of trees surrounding it. But from the back, the house looked naked, as though completely open to the forest and fields and the creek beyond—a mecca for the creeping, crawling things of the night.

Lynn laughed a little to herself. Now *that* was imaginative nonsense—"creeping crawling things of the night." That was "purple prose" as Mother called it, when a writer went overboard describing something. Nevertheless, from every conceivable angle, the Tuggle house was not like the other houses on the street. It was very much alone, isolated—a house of secrets among the thorn apple trees.

There had indeed been a windstorm. Here and there

Lynn saw a limb down in a neighboring yard, or a piece of fencing that had blown over. But the worst damage had been done to the Tuggle house. Was it because hers was the highest house on the hill, subject to the full force of the wind? Or was there another reason? When did the storm peak? Lynn wondered—shortly after midnight, at the death of the lead crow, perhaps? Was it possible that at the death of the bird demon, the power that Mrs. Tuggle had directed toward Mouse and Lynn had turned back on herself?

As Lynn entered the yard, between the old barn and Mother's studio, she saw the trunk of a large locust tree, which had grazed Mrs. Tuggle's roof as it fell and now lay across her back steps. One window had been broken, and there were shingles and splinters of wood strewn about on the ground.

Lynn went around to the front door, stepped up on the porch, and grasped the ugly troll-like door knocker firmly. She rapped it twice, and then—in a bold display of nerve—simply opened the door herself and entered the dark hallway.

There were footsteps at the other end, and Mrs. Morley appeared in the kitchen doorway.

"Lynn! My goodness, you're up early! I expected that you girls would sleep till noon."

"I heard what happened and thought I'd come by to see if I could help," Lynn said, choosing the words carefully. She remembered at the same time that Mother had suggested she stay away from Mrs. Tuggle's house, but she must have sounded so inwardly strong and mature that Mrs. Morley decided she could handle it.

"Well, I'm sure we could find something for you! I've just washed a sinkful of dishes that were thick with plaster dust, and you could dry them for us. . . ."

Lynn walked on down the hall, past the old clock with one hand missing that ticked no longer, the un-smiling photos of Tuggle relatives there on the wall, the deacon's bench with the frayed velvet cushion, the cracked vase, the coat tree with hooks that looked like claws. . . .

The kitchen was grimy with plaster that had fallen from one corner. The table was covered with dishes that had been removed from an open cupboard and were waiting their turn in the sink.

Mrs. Tuggle was standing with her back to them, sweeping up a pile of wood splinters. Hearing the footsteps, she turned slowly around and her eyes met Lynn's.

Lynn stared. They did not seem like Mrs. Tuggle's eyes at all, but rather the eyes of a crow. The green eye—the gray one even—both had a strange yellow cast to them as though they had undergone a color change during the night; and her nose, angular enough before, looked even sharper now, like the beak of a bird. Had she always looked this way? Had Lynn never noticed it before? Didn't Mother notice?

"Lynn's come to help out a bit," Mother said to the old woman. "You know, Mrs. Tuggle, you don't look so good this morning. You must be awfully tired. Why don't you sit down and rest awhile?"

Mrs. Tuggle did not take her eyes off Lynn.

"I'm quite all right," she said, and Lynn could not decide if her expression was one of curiosity or anger. "I feel better up and about than I do in a chair."

"Then *I'm* going to get off *my* feet for a bit," Mother said, sitting down in the rocking chair near the table. "There's no room for any more dishes in the rinse pan anyway, so I'll just wait till Lynn's dried a few."

Lynn reached for the towel, looking Mrs. Tuggle straight in the eye all the while. She would not be scared down or stared down, and she wanted the old woman to know it.

"Strange that you had such a wind here last night, Mrs. Tuggle," she said boldly. "I didn't hear it at all."

"Didn't you, now?"

"No. Mouse and I were up quite late," Lynn continued recklessly, "and except for a little breeze that blew in like a melody, we didn't notice a strong wind at all."

"Which reminds me," said Mother, her feet up on a kitchen chair as she rocked herself, "I've reached a point

175

in my manuscript where I need a song or a chant or something to fill in—something suitable for witches to sing. You told me one, Lynn, that you said Mrs. Tuggle had sung to you. What was it again?"

"I remember it very well," said Lynn, and her voice was strong as she recited the words:

> "Sing of morning, sing of noon,
> Sing of evening's silver moon,
> Feel the darkness, touch the black
> Hear the shadows whisper back.

"Isn't that the way it goes, Mrs. Tuggle?"

Mrs. Tuggle frowned. "Yes, child, that's the way it goes."

"Beautiful!" Mrs. Morley clapped her hands delightedly. "Just what I need. You see, this girl in my story is trapped in a. . . . Oh, I'd better not talk about it. Somehow it always ruins things when I do. No, I'll just wait till the book is all finished and read it to you then."

At that moment there was a noise outside and a shadow fell on the floor. An instant later, the cat leaped down from the broken window and dropped to the linoleum, its fur damp and bedraggled. When it saw Lynn it hissed loudly and backed away, its tail swishing.

Lynn stared. The cat was alive. She hadn't killed it

after all. Somehow it had survived the water and the rocks and the current and made its way back.

"What's happened to the poor animal?" Mrs. Morley said, and stopped rocking. "Why, look at him! He's not used to seeing Lynn here, is he? Maybe he blames her for all the mess and confusion!"

Mrs. Tuggle fixed her gaze on Lynn. This time the eyes glared angrily out from beneath her black bushy brows, and they had the look of rage.

"Aye, looks like someone tried to rid old Mrs. Tuggle of her cat, but 'tis nine lives the animal has, and more besides." She laughed then, and her laughter reverberated through the high-ceilinged rooms like the staccato roll of a drum.

For just a brief moment, Lynn felt a trace of fear. Then the strength she had experienced that morning surged back again, even stronger, and she felt that no matter what Mrs. Tuggle might try again, if indeed she tried anything at all, Lynn would be ready. It was time to show the old woman that it did not matter whether the cat were alive or dead. She would not let it affect her, or Marjorie either.

And so she looked directly at the cat and said, in a sing-song voice, as though talking to herself:

"Feel the darkness, touch the black,
Hear the shadows whisper back."

In response, the cat leaped, but not for Lynn. It

landed lightly in Mrs. Morley's lap, surprising Mother as much as it surprised Lynn.

"So you want to be rocked, do you?" Mrs. Morley said, stroking its head. "I don't blame you. If I looked as awful as you do this morning, Cat, I'd want to be rocked too."

With a strange cat-smile on its face, the animal made a nest for itself there on Mother's skirt and settled down. And the rocking chair began to move, back and forth, back and forth, as Mother smoothed the cat's ruffled fur.

It knows better than to tangle with me, Lynn thought with satisfaction as she picked up the dish towel and began wiping a saucer. *But just let it try . . . just let it try!* She faced the cat as she worked, glad that she could look into its eyes without fearing it any longer.

There was no other talk for a while, just the occasional clink and thud of kitchen noises and the squeak of the rocking chair. Then, from deep in the cat's throat, came a low, defiant rattling sort of purr, like a teakettle full of stones simmering somewhere on a dusty hearth.

Hearing the purr, Lynn began to hum the tune that Mrs. Tuggle often sang—hummed it right back in the cat's face, afraid of nothing.

Mrs. Tuggle, watching from the corner, nodded slightly to herself and smiled. And as her thin lips parted, her eyes shone yellow once more, and the gold tooth gleamed from the darkness of her mouth.